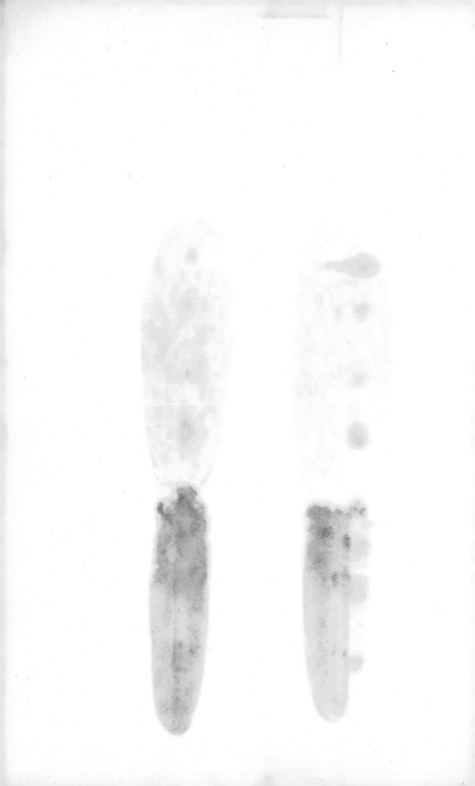

Dvora's Journey

MARGE BLAINE

DVORA'S JOURNEY

Illustrated by
Gabriel Lisowski

Holt, Rinehart and Winston
New York

Text copyright © 1979 by Marge Blaine
Illustrations copyright © 1979 by Gabriel Lisowski
All rights reserved, including the right to reproduce
this book or portions thereof in any form.
Published simultaneously in Canada by Holt, Rinehart
and Winston of Canada, Limited
Printed in the United States of America

10 9 8 7 6 5 4 3 2 1

Library of Congress Cataloging in Publication Data
Blaine, Marge. Dvora's journey.
    SUMMARY: After fleeing from Russia in 1904,
12-year-old Dvora and her family face
unexpected problems.
    [1. Jews—Fiction. 2. Refugees—Fiction.
3. Family life—Fiction] I. Title.
PZ7.B5372Dv   [Fic]   78-26349
ISBN 0-03-048306-9

To my father,
Louis Bendis, who made the journey too.

Contents

1. Cossacks in the Woods   9

2. Papa's Plan   19

3. The Treasure Chest   29

4. Market Day   38

5. The Dream   48

6. Stealing the Border   60

7. By Train across Poland   69

8. Welcome to Germany!   80

9. Loss   91

10. Hamburg   105

11. The Telegram   111

12. Crossing Over   119

1.

Cossacks in the Woods

Tillie and I were on the way back to town, our arms filled with firewood, when we saw the horsemen.

"Dvora! Look!" Tillie whispered, pointing ahead. "Who do you think they are?"

"I'm not sure," I told her. "They look like soldiers. Cossacks maybe."

"Do you think we should hide?"

"Better not. They've probably already seen us. Just keep on walking. And try not to look scared."

"I am scared," Tillie cried.

"I am too, a little. But we'd better not let *them* see that. Remember what happened to Abraham."

"All right, Dvora. I'll try, but it won't be easy."

As we drew closer, Tillie and I pulled our shawls more tightly around our shoulders and walked

9

quickly to show we weren't afraid. I could feel my cheeks grow hot and my heart pound. "What will I do if they try to talk to us or stop us?" I wondered. I thought of stories I'd heard about what happened to girls in other villages when soldiers caught them in the woods.

It seemed forever until we got to where they were, but finally we passed them. I drew a deep breath. Just then one of the soldiers laughed and called to the others. They wheeled their horses back onto the path, kicking them into a gallop.

"Watch out, girlie!" the leader called as they rode by. Tillie and I tried to act as though we hadn't heard, keeping our eyes straight ahead until they were out of sight. We waited for the thick cloud of dust they'd raised to settle.

"Thank goodness they've gone," I gasped. "We can slow down now. I'm all out of breath."

Tillie shook her head. "We still have to hurry," she said. "It's getting late and my mother needs the wood."

I looked at the sun. It was almost at the edge of the sky. I could see the red glow where it was about to disappear into the trees. "Yes. We'd better hurry. My mother will worry if I'm not home before dark."

"You'll be there in time," Tillie said. "See, there's the first house."

The first house wasn't more than a tumbledown

shack. I'd always hated walking past it. A dog barked but no one was in sight.

As we walked farther down the road we could see people inside some of the houses getting ready for dinner. "How come your mother waited so late to send you for wood?" I asked Tillie.

"I was busy, Dvora. You know I was at the market all morning."

"Why did she have to send you then? Couldn't one of your sisters go instead? You have to do everything!"

"I don't do everything. Mama does the cooking and takes care of the house and baby. And my sisters help her."

"Well, you do *almost* everything. You're the one who works at the market. You do all the shopping. And she makes you get the firewood too."

Tillie shrugged. "I guess it's because I'm the only one with a head on her shoulders."

"What do you mean?"

"If you sent Rachel or Yettie for firewood they'd bring home leaves or flowers instead. And can you imagine Sara at the market?" She imitated her sister's high, whiny voice: "Oh, you haven't enough for the broom? Well, that's all right. Just give me two kopeks then." Tillie looked at me. "Never mind that the straw alone is worth more than two kopeks," she added.

"I see what you mean, but it still doesn't seem fair."

"Fair, shmair. Who cares about fair when you're hungry?" Tillie sounded almost angry and began to walk more quickly.

Poor Tillie. I wondered what it must be like to live in her house. It had a sour smell, a combination of stale food and dirty clothing.

Her mother was always scolding Tillie or one of her sisters and criticizing their work.

Tillie's father was hardly home except to eat. He spent his time complaining: "Four girls. Four girls. What did I ever do to deserve such luck? What can you do with girls? No help earning a living and next thing you know they'll be needing a dowry. Girls!"

My father would never talk like that even if he had all girls—which he didn't.

"Well! It's about time!" Tillie's mother screeched as soon as she saw us. "What took you so long? The cooking fire's almost out!"

"I'm sorry, Mama," Tillie said. "We hurried as fast as we could, but it's a long walk."

"You never do anything right," her mother muttered. "Probably spent all your time fooling around. That's why you're late."

Tillie rolled her eyes at me as if to ask, "Did you ever hear anyone like Mama?" She dumped her load of wood next to the oven, and I added mine to the pile.

"That ought to be enough for a few days," I whispered to her.

"Yes. I'm glad winter's over. We need less wood now. Thanks for helping, Dvora. And don't let Mama bother you. It's just her way."

"I know."

"Oh, Mama," Tillie said. "We saw some soldiers today. They rode right by us and into town. We were afraid they'd stop us."

"You keep away from soldiers, young lady," her mother warned. "I don't want you getting into trouble."

Tillie sighed. "Yes, Mama."

"We kept out of their way, Mrs. Levy," I told her, walking toward the door. "Goodbye. I have to go now. My mother will be wondering where I am."

"Bye, Dvora," Tillie called. Her mother nodded, not saying anything. As soon as I was gone, I heard her begin to grumble to Tillie again about supper. "Poor Tillie," I thought again. "She tries so hard to please, but her mother's never satisfied. I don't know how she can stand it."

I ran quickly down the street and around the corner to our courtyard. My mother had lit the lamps already. I could see figures moving inside in the orange light.

"Hello, Mama," I called, opening the door.

"Dvora," Mama said, turning from the stove. "I'm glad you're home. I was just beginning to worry."

"I didn't realize it was so late," I told her. "Tillie went for firewood so I helped her."

My mother sighed. "That poor child has to work so hard. It's a shame."

"What are you making, Mama?" I asked. "It smells delicious!"

"Just a meat soup."

"Meat soup! That's what Mama calls it." My older sister, Rivkeh, laughed. "But it's more than just meat. You know Mama's soups: a little of this, a little of that, meat, chicken, vegetables, spices. Even I don't know everything she puts into the pot."

"Can I help?"

My mother glanced at Rivkeh, who'd almost finished setting the table, and at Minnie and Yossel, who were playing quietly in the corner.

"We're almost ready here," she said. "But you can go next door and call Papa. He'll need time to wash up before we eat."

"Saul," I heard her call to my big brother as I went out again, "put your books away now. You'll finish studying later."

Soon we sat down at the table Rivkeh had set so carefully, Papa in his chair at the head, Saul and Rivkeh on either side of him, the rest of us on the benches. Mama sat closest to the stove. There was a plate of freshly baked challah and a dish of homemade jam in the center of the table where everyone could reach it. In front of each place was a wooden soup bowl, a big spoon, and an embroidered napkin.

"Are you ready, Jacob?" Mama asked.

Papa nodded and passed her his bowl. I looked at his arms, muscled from his work. "I'm glad he's so strong," I thought, "not a skinny little man with a mean face like Tillie's father."

Mama filled his plate from the soup pot on the stove and we passed it back down the table to Papa. I glanced at the chunks of beef, carrots, turnips, and potatoes in the thick gravy as it went by. Oh, did it smell good! I could hardly wait to eat, but Mama served Saul next and then Rivkeh before it was my turn.

When we'd all been served, Papa made the prayer. Soon everyone was busy eating, passing the plate of bread back and forth. I liked dinner time, the whole family sitting down together, not like at Tillie's house where they just crowded around and ate from the pot.

"Well," Papa said, sopping up what was left of his soup with some bread, "I heard some news in the shop today."

"What is it, Jacob?" Mama asked.

"The Czar is sending soldiers here," Papa said. "They have a quota to fill by the end of the month, and it's higher than ever before."

"What's a quota?" Rivkeh asked at the same time Saul said, "I heard about it in school today. A lot of the boys are afraid they'll be taken."

I wanted to tell them I'd seen the soldiers, but I knew I'd have to wait.

"The Czar needs men for his army," my father started to explain. "Sometimes they get enough volunteers."

"Why would anyone volunteer?" Saul asked.

"Well, it's a pretty good job, for someone who doesn't have a trade or much of an education," Papa explained. "It pays pretty well too. Only there isn't much of a future in it, especially if there's a war on."

"Is there a war on now?" Yossel asked.

"No, but the army isn't a good place for a Jewish boy. The other soldiers take advantage of the Jews, give them the worst jobs. And there's no way to get kosher food."

"I wouldn't want to go into the army anyway," Saul said. "You promised I could finish school and study at the university."

"I know," Papa said. "I've been saving money to pay someone to take your place in case you were called—there's usually a peasant boy who's glad enough of the money—except that the law's just been changed. If they call you now, you must go. No more substitutes."

"Do you think they'll take me?" Saul asked anxiously. "I'm not even fourteen yet."

"I don't know. I'm afraid they may. And if they don't try this month, they'll get around to you soon enough. Only we won't let them."

"I don't want to be in the army," Saul announced. "I'll do anything you say."

"Me too!" Yossel added.

"You're too young!" Minnie told him. "You're only six."

"Well, I wouldn't want to go anyway. Besides I'll be old enough in a few years."

"Children! Children! Shush," Mama said. "Your father hasn't finished."

"There are a few things that can be done," Papa continued. "Sometimes a boy will injure himself to keep out of the army, cut off some toes or even a hand. They won't take a cripple."

Saul tried to look as though he weren't upset, but I could tell from his eyes that he was scared. "Are you joking, Papa?" I asked.

"No. I'm not joking. I didn't say Saul *should* do it, just that some boys do, to keep from going into the army and getting killed." He paused. "I think it would be better than joining."

I looked down the table at Saul, my handsome brother. His hands lay on the table next to his empty soup bowl, the fingers curved slightly. I couldn't bear the thought of anyone cutting off his fingers. He'd be a cripple for life!

But if he were killed? That would be the end of his life.

"What was the other idea you had, Papa?" Saul finally asked.

"Another way is to hide," Papa said. "Boys try hiding in the woods or in another town. Only that isn't so good either. You can't hide forever."

"Then what will I do?"

My father smiled. I could see he had another plan, one that wouldn't mean hurting Saul. I could hardly wait to hear what it was.

2.

Papa's Plan

Papa leaned back in his chair. Rivkeh, Saul, and I waited to hear what he had to say. Even Minnie and Yossel were still for once.

"What is it, Papa?" I finally asked. "What's the other plan for Saul?"

"It's a big change," my father said slowly. "And it isn't just for Saul. It's for all of us."

"All of us? What do you mean?" Did Papa want us all to join the army and help Saul? Or would we hide him in the woods from the soldiers? Maybe Papa had decided to tell them that Yossel was Saul and was too young to go into the army.

Finally Papa spoke. "Do you remember the Zimmermans?" he asked.

"Yes," Saul said. "I knew Isaac from cheder. He was a year older than me."

"Ruthie and Tillie and I were best friends since we were little," I added. "I never knew what happened to Ruthie . . . all of a sudden she just went away."

My father nodded. "They left town," he said. "Let me see, it must have been two or three years ago, 1901 or 1902. Only they didn't move away." He paused. "They went to America."

"America?" Minnie asked.

"Yes. Mr. Zimmerman had two brothers there. They wrote they could get him a good job, working in the pants factory with them. They said he could make twenty rubles a week."

"That's a fortune!" Saul exclaimed.

"Well, maybe they were exaggerating a little. I don't know. Anyway, they decided to go. They didn't tell too many people because they were afraid the soldiers would try to stop them."

"What does that have to do with us?" Saul asked.

Mama sat quietly in her chair, her eyes fixed on Papa. I think she knew what he was going to say.

"We're going to leave Russia," Papa announced. "We're going to America too!"

"Go to America?"

"Leave here?"

"When?"

"How can we?"

All of us began asking questions at once.

"Shush! One at a time. I can't even hear when

you're all talking." Papa pointed to Rivkeh. "You're the oldest. You first."

"Do you mean everyone?" she asked.

"Yes," Papa nodded. "Everyone."

"Couldn't just Saul go? He's the one who has to go into the army."

"Yes," Papa said slowly. "I guess we could just send Saul. But we're a family. If we sent Saul, we'd never see him again, and our family wouldn't be the same. Besides, before we know it, Yossel will be old enough for the army too."

"Papa!" I cried. "This is so sudden. You never said anything about it before."

"Not to you, but Mama and I have been talking about America for years. Even before the Zimmermans went."

"How come you didn't tell us?"

"We wanted to wait until we were sure," Papa explained. "Do you remember your mother's brother, Shmuel? He's been in America a long time. Shmuel's written to Mama, urging us to come. He says he'll help us get settled."

I wasn't sure if I knew who Uncle Shmuel was. I remembered a man with a loud voice, fingers pinching my cheek and someone saying, "Give us a smile, Dvora, that's a good girl." I hadn't liked him very much; his fingers hurt. Could that have been Uncle Shmuel?

"What about cheder and the university, Papa?" Saul wanted to know. "Will I be able to study in America?"

"That's another reason we want to go," Papa told him. "Children can all go to school there, even Jewish children. And it's free."

"Free?"

"Yes. That's what we've been told." All of us were quiet, thinking that over.

"There are many opportunities for good workers like your father. They need people who can build and make things," said Mama, who hadn't spoken until now.

"Any more questions?"

"Where is America?" Minnie asked. "And how do we get there?"

"What a dumb question!" I said. "You're such a baby!" But I wasn't sure myself. All I knew was that my friend Ruthie lived there. Maybe going to America was like dying. Someone dies and you never see them again. Ruthie had gone to America and I never saw her either.

"That's not a silly question," my father told Minnie. "And you know better than to talk that way to your sister!" he reminded me.

Papa looked down the table, at each of us in turn. "America is another country," he began.

"What's a country?" Yossel asked.

"It's a place where people live, just like Russia," Saul told him. "Now stop interrupting Papa or he'll never finish!"

"There are a lot of stories about America," Papa told us. "And I'm not sure which of them are true. People say you can find gold in the streets there." Minnie's eyes opened wide at that. She loved jewelry, especially her gold locket, and she was always asking to wear Mama's gold earrings.

"I don't know whether that's true," Papa continued, "but I do know that there are plenty of jobs. And everyone can go to school: rich, poor, Jew, gentile, everyone. Not like here. It's a place where a man can begin a new life."

Papa nodded. "Mama and I have been thinking about it for a long time. My customers have trouble paying me for the work I've done. Taxes are getting higher and higher. And now this news about the army. Yes," he finished, "we're going to America."

For once no one said anything. There was so much to think about. Saul was probably wondering about the kinds of schools he'd find in America. And Rivkeh about the husband Papa would find for her there. Minnie would be thinking about what to do with all the gold she'd find on the streets, and Yossel about beginning cheder.

My own head was in a whirl. One part of me wanted to go, to be with my family, to see the place called America and what it was really like.

But leaving would be terrible. I wasn't at all sure I wanted to go. How could I leave this house, the only home I'd ever had? The village where I'd lived all my life? My school? Everything? And what would Tillie do without me? She'd have no one, no one at all. It would be even worse for her than for me.

And for what? A place I'd never seen and never even heard of before now. Papa said there'd be schools there, but how did he know there'd be one for me? I'd been promised a place in the girls' high school for next year. What if there was no school for twelve-year-old girls in America? Would I have to leave school the way Rivkeh did when she was my age? What would happen to me then? I knew I would never be able to just stay home and help Mama the way Rivkeh did.

"Come girls, clear the table." Mama's voice interrupted my thoughts. "It's getting late. And Saul, take the other lamp to the corner so you can finish studying."

Mama led Minnie and Yossel to the back rooms. I could hear her helping them get ready for bed. Minnie was crying, "I don't want to go. I don't want to go." I felt almost like crying, too.

I began to stack up the soup bowls. Papa had carved some of them before I was born. He'd made one for each of us as soon as we were old enough to sit at the table with the family.

I ran my fingers over the polished wood. Papa did

such fine work. Would we take these with us to America?

Rivkeh and I stacked the dishes in the pan, and I poured water over them. "Let them soak for a few minutes," Rivkeh told me. "We were at the table so long tonight."

We put the bread and jam back into the cupboard. Rivkeh took a broom and swept the floor while I went outside and shook the crumbs out of the cloth.

"Do you think we'll really go?" Rivkeh asked as we washed the dishes and put them away.

"Papa says so. Do you want to?"

"I'm not sure," Rivkeh said. "It's so sudden. Still we have no other choice."

"I know. But it's hard to think of leaving. There's so much we'll miss."

When we were done, we kissed Mama and Papa goodnight. "Now remember," Papa warned, "don't tell anyone about our plans."

"Why not?"

"If the army knew we were trying to leave, they'd stop us. They'd put Saul in the army and take me to jail for helping him get away."

I shivered. "What about Tillie?" I asked. "Can't I just tell her? She doesn't know any soldiers."

"No," Papa sighed, "only she'd probably tell her

parents. And her father is just the kind to turn us in. There's a reward for news like that."

"Won't I even be able to say goodbye? Will I have to leave my very best friend without saying *anything* to her?"

"You'll be able to say goodbye," Papa said. "Just before we leave. When it would be too late for anyone to stop us. But don't tell her now."

"I won't, Papa," I said. "Goodnight."

Rivkeh and I went to the bedroom. Minnie lay spread out across the bed we shared. Her clothes, as usual, were in a heap on the floor. Rivkeh sighed and bent to pick them up.

After she hung Minnie's things on the hook next to the bed, Rivkeh took her nightdress and went behind the curtain. Rivkeh had always been modest, but ever since she'd begun changing into a woman, she never let anyone see her undress.

I knew she had breasts, because I could see them under her dresses. Sometimes I'd feel their softness at night when I turned against her in bed. I looked down at my own flat chest. "I wonder when I'll get my woman's body," I thought. "I'm twelve already. Rivkeh started earlier than that."

I poured some water into the basin and washed my face, drying it carefully with a soft towel. I undid my braids and shook my hair free over my shoulders. I wished Mama would let me wear it loose. It was thick and silky but I had to wear it tightly braided all day.

Rivkeh and I climbed into bed, pushing Minnie to one side. "Goodnight," I whispered.

"Goodnight."

Soon Rivkeh seemed to be asleep. I could hear her quiet breathing. But I couldn't sleep. Minnie's sharp elbow poked me in the back. In the other room my parents' voices went on and on.

As I lay there, I wondered what it would be like to go to America. I thought of the soldiers I'd seen earlier in the day. If they knew we were trying to leave, they'd stop us—or worse.

"I wish I didn't have to go," I thought. "Yet if we do, I hope we get away safely."

I finally fell asleep thinking, "Maybe we'll live near Ruthie in America. She can show me all around. We'll go to school together . . . and tell secrets . . . just the way we used to. After school we'll go picking wildflowers in the forest . . . or gold in the streets . . . or whatever they do after school in America."

3.

The Treasure Chest

There was so much to do during the next few days, I almost forgot my worries about leaving.

Mama began cleaning the house as though we were getting ready for a party instead of a journey. Rivkeh helped, airing out featherbeds, beating the rugs, and scrubbing the cooking pots. They even washed all the walls.

One morning Mama called Rivkeh to the big chest where we kept our best things. They began piling our treasures on the bed: extra featherbeds, embroidered tablecloths, shawls, an old prayer book, and bed linens. I wondered what they were doing. I loved looking through the chest, touching the old quilts Mama's mother had given her, imagining what Mama's life was like when she was a girl.

"Dvora!" Mama called. "Minnie! Leave the rest of

the dishes and come here. There's something I want you to do."

"What is it?" I asked, fingering the soft shawl on top of the pile.

"We have to decide what we're taking with us."

"But these are our treasures," I said. "You've been saving them for us, for when we grow up and have homes of our own."

"I know, Dvora," Mama said sadly, "but we can't take everything with us."

"Why not?" Minnie asked.

"We have to carry whatever we take . . . all the way to America. Papa needs tools so he'll be able to work there. We need clothing for each of us, bedding, and cooking pots too."

"What about the rest?"

"We'll sell some of it at the market. We can use all the money we can lay our hands on for the trip. Anything we can't sell we'll give away, or leave here."

Mama turned to the enormous stack of featherbeds. "Each of you pick one," she said. "The one you want to take to America."

Minnie's eyes lit up. "Can I have this one?" she asked, pointing to the fanciest. It was made of silk, with beautiful colors, only it wasn't very thick. "It's the prettiest!"

Mama nodded. "Take it." She reached down

again. "Here's the quilt your grandma helped me make when I was your age, Rivkeh," Mama said, stroking it. "Do you want it for your dowry?" The colors were a little faded and it was worn in one corner, but the embroidery was still good.

Rivkeh shook her head. "It's nice, Mama," she said, but if I have to choose just one, I'd rather have a new quilt, one you and I made."

Mama took the old quilt and started to put it with the things we were leaving.

"Can I have it, Mama?" I asked. "I've always loved that quilt, only it was supposed to be Rivkeh's."

"I guess so, Dvora, if that's what you want. Are you sure? I made the blue one specially for you."

I looked at the two quilts. "I wish we weren't going!" I thought angrily. "Then we could keep everything. How can I choose? It just isn't fair!" Only I didn't say that to Mama.

"It's hard to choose, Mama," I finally said. "I like them both, but if I have to take just one, let me have the old quilt."

"You really are a one for old things, Dvora." Mama smiled. "Yet there won't be many old things where we're going, so perhaps it's just as well. I'll try to pack them both—if there's room."

We spent almost the whole morning sorting through the chest. When we'd finished, there was a small pile for each of us to take and a much larger one in the middle of the floor. "I wish we didn't have to leave all that," Rivkeh sighed.

"I know. I feel the same way," I told her.

"Well, there's nothing to be done about it, girls," Mama said briskly. "There's an old saying, 'I will pawn my featherbeds to achieve my goal.' That's all we're doing."

"But it doesn't say anything about shawls and blouses and skirts! We're leaving almost *everything*!"

"That can't be helped," Mama said. "We're almost finished, except for this." She pointed to the small wooden box which held our jewelry. Papa had made it for her when they were first married.

"Aren't we taking all the jewelry, Mama?" Minnie asked. "The box isn't very big."

"Or heavy either," I added.

"No," Mama agreed. "It isn't big or heavy, but we can't take all the jewelry anyway."

"Why not?" Minnie sounded worried.

"We need all the money we can get for the trip. Papa's been saving for a long time, still we want as much as possible. The jewelry should be worth a lot."

"Do you have to sell it all?" Minnie cried. "What about my locket—and the gold earrings? You can't sell those!"

"Not the earrings," Mama told her. "I didn't say we'd sell it *all*. And we won't sell the locket either, not unless we get a very good price, at least four rubles."

"I hope no one wants it!" Minnie shouted.

"Dvora will take some things to the market next Thursday when Tillie goes," Mama said. "We'll see what happens."

Minnie was upset. The locket meant a lot to her, probably as much as the old quilt did to me.

"Don't worry, Minnie," I told her. "Maybe no one will buy it. Besides, if they do, we can get you another in America when we're rich."

"Even if they do have gold in America, they won't have anything like my locket!"

"All right, girls. That's enough," Mama said. "Go outside now and find something to do. Rivkeh and I have to do the washing."

"Didn't you just wash yesterday?" I asked.

"We want everything to be clean, for America," Mama said. Rivkeh began to fill the tub.

"I know why she's Mama's favorite," I said to myself on the way out. "She always says 'Yes, Mama' instead of 'Why?' or 'How come?' the way I do. And she's good *all* the time."

Minnie ran off to find Yossel. No one was out on our street and I wanted to talk to someone. I was afraid to see Tillie; it would be too hard not telling her we were leaving.

Then I thought of Papa. I ran around the back to

his workshop. I could hear the sound of his hammer as I reached the door.

"Papa," I called from the doorway. "Can I come in?"

"Dvora? Of course. It's been a long time since you've come to the shop."

"Well, I've been busy."

"I know. That's what happens as one gets older!" My father wore his black work apron. There were pockets in the front. I could see a mallet and a small chisel sticking out.

"What are you making?" I asked.

"I promised Mrs. Wasserman I'd try to fix this," he explained, pointing to the chair on the work-bench. "I don't want any work unfinished when we leave." The chair was in two parts, the pins that held the front to the back splintered.

"Can I help?"

"That will be like old times," my father said, "You used to come and help me all the time when you were younger!" He handed me the new pins he'd carved. "Take the sandpaper and see if you can make these completely smooth."

Papa fit a small bit into his drill. Then he made new holes in both halves of the chair. I polished the pins until there was no roughness left and gave them to my father.

Papa ran his finger along the edge. "Very good,

Dvora, they'll fit perfectly. Too bad you weren't a boy. You'd have made a good carpenter."

I'd always loved the shop: the smell of the wood, paints, and glue. When I was little I used to watch Papa work and talk with him. I used to think he liked me best—he'd talk with me the most. Sometimes I think he still does. At least he likes me best of all his daughters.

Papa turned back to the chair and fit the pins into the holes. "Perfect!" he announced. He spread glue carefully over both ends of the pins and put them into the front half of the chair. Then, just as carefully, he fitted the back of the chair on. "There. That does it." He took a rag and wiped off some glue that had squeezed out, wiped his hand, and put a clamp around the legs of the chair.

"Tomorrow that chair will be as good as new," he told me. "Thanks for helping. It's nice having you here."

"And I like being here, Papa." I waited until he looked up. "I guess we won't be doing it anymore."

"Not here, anyway."

"Will you have a shop in America?"

"I don't know," he said. "I hope so."

"What about me, Papa?" I asked. "What about me?" I wanted to tell him what had been worrying me ever since he'd told us we were leaving.

"What do you mean, Dvora?"

"What will *I* do in America?"

"I don't understand."

"Well, Mama will take care of the house, the way she does here. You have your work. Saul will go to school and Rivkeh will be getting married soon, the way you've always planned for her. But what will I do in America?"

"Why won't it be the same for you?"

"I'm supposed to go to the special high school next year," I reminded him, "to learn Russian, maybe become a teacher in a girls' school."

"Yes. That's what we planned. You're a good student. The melamed said so," my father agreed.

"But they won't teach Russian in America, will they Papa?"

"No, I guess not."

I leaned on Papa's shoulder. It felt good, strong and comfortable. "Will I go to school in America, Papa? Will I learn to read in American and talk American? That's what I've been worrying about."

"If there are high schools for girls, Dvora, you'll go. I promise you."

"What if there aren't?"

My father shrugged. "We'll see what smart girls do there. Maybe you'll be a carpenter, an American carpenter. Or maybe they'll let you be the President, like George Washington. We'll see," he told me. "We'll just have to wait and see."

4.

Market Day

"**D**vora! Dvora! Wake up!" It was still dark, but Mama kept shaking me. "Dvora," she said again. "Get up or you'll be late."

"What's the matter, Mama?" I asked sleepily. "It's still early. The water carrier hasn't even come yet."

"Don't you remember? It's Thursday. Today's market day. You said you'd go with Tillie."

"I'm sorry, Mama. I guess I forgot."

"Now hurry and get dressed."

I slipped out of bed without waking Rivkeh or Minnie and ate the breakfast Mama had waiting for me on the table. A bundle, containing some shawls, a few of Papa's small carvings, embroideries, and Minnie's locket, was at the door.

"Are you sure you'll be all right?" Mama asked anxiously.

"Don't be silly, Mama. I used to go to market all

the time with Tillie last summer when I didn't have school. I love it there!"

"But you never tried to sell anything before."

"Tillie will help me if I have any trouble. Only I won't. You'll see."

Mama kissed me. "Have a good day, Dvora."

"Oh, Mama. What should I tell Tillie? She'll wonder why I'm selling all this."

Mama thought for a moment. "Just say we're a little short. That we need the money for Saul's education."

"I will. That's almost the truth anyway." I met Tillie at the corner. She had the straw parts of the brooms balanced on her head, the handles in one hand, and a white package in the other.

"How can you carry all that?" I asked her.

She shrugged. "I do it every week. Come on. We're going to be late."

"It's still early."

"The best spots get taken first. I won't do as well if I'm in the back." Tillie sounded worried. I knew her family depended on the money she brought home from market. Even though she was just my age, she was the one who earned the most money.

We turned into the main street and joined the people walking to market. As we got closer to the end of town, it got more and more crowded. There were people from the village and peasants from the

surrounding area. Almost everyone was carrying
something: stacks of soap, trays of breads, candles,
fabrics, and sacks of vegetables. Those who didn't
had empty baskets in which they'd put their pur-
chases.

We were almost at the entrance when someone
called, "Look out!" A group of soldiers came gallop-
ing down the street, their horses' hooves churning
up a cloud of dust. People pushed wildly to get out
of the way. I almost dropped my bundle, but the
men behind us helped us to the side.

"Why don't they look where they're going?" one of
them complained.

"Them!" The other man spat into the street.
"They can do whatever they want. It's up to us to
keep out of their way!"

Finally we reached the market. We passed the
herring stall where a bent old man sold pickled and
smoked herring. He'd been there ever since I could
remember, just as old when I was a little girl as he
seemed now.

There were rows of peasant women, piles of fresh
plump carrots, turnips, and potatoes on the ground
in front of them.

I could see the poultry woman near the end of the
row. Her chickens crouched near her skirts, their
heads hidden under their feathers. Each chicken
had a loop of string tied around its legs so it couldn't

escape and a longer string tied all the birds together.

The old woman called, "Chicken for sale! Plump tender birds! Buy your chickens now!" When a purchaser stopped, the woman pulled on the long cord. All the birds woke up crying "Sqquuaaaak! SQQUUAAAAK!"

"Let's stay here," Tillie said, pointing to an empty stall not far from the poultry woman.

"Do we have to? I'd rather be farther in."

"It's best to be near the doorway," Tillie explained. "Brooms are too big to carry around. People like to buy them on their way out."

Tillie untied her bundles. She propped the broom handles up in rows in front of the stall. The straw ends she set out on the wooden stand along with some knitted caps and scarves from her other package.

"Aren't you going to put out your things?" she asked me.

I looked up with a start. "I can't seem to do anything right today," I told her.

"Your mind must be somewhere else."

"You're right." My mind *was* somewhere else—on the way to America to be exact, but I couldn't tell that to Tillie. How I wished I could talk to her, tell her how worried I was about what was going to happen to me. About what it would be like in America. Even if Tillie didn't know, talking would have helped, but Papa said I couldn't. Slowly I undid my bundle and set out my clothes.

Despite what Tillie had said about people buying brooms on their way out, her first customer was a woman who worked at the market. The old woman who sold herbs and tea bought one to sweep in front of her stall.

Business was good during the morning. Many people stopped for brooms. Each time Tillie bargained with them about the price, asking about twice what she really wanted, finally settling for what she'd planned on. Before the purchaser left, Tillie took a piece of heavy twine and lashed the straw part of the broom to the handle, ending it off with a deft knot. I sold some of the embroideries I'd brought too. Most of the women looked at my gold locket before they left, but the price Mama wanted was too high for them to even begin to bargain.

At noon, while Tillie and I ate the lunches we'd brought, I watched the old woman with the chickens. Someone stopped and looked carefully at the birds. Did this one have a patch where feathers were missing? Did that one have a bad eye? Which would make the tastiest stew for Shabbas dinner? The bargaining took a long time. Finally the seller cut the string connecting the bird to the others and handed it to the new owner.

"I hate when a chicken leaves the market," I told Tillie.

She shrugged. "Why? They have to be sold, don't they?"

"They scream so. Sometimes I think they know what's going to happen!"

"Oh, don't be silly. Chickens don't know anything."

"I'm not silly. Their squawk is terrible."

"I guess it is pretty loud," she agreed.

"Sometimes I feel as though I'm a chicken," I said, "That someone's going to chop off my head and eat me!"

Tillie shook her head in sympathy, but I could see she didn't really understand what I meant.

It grew hotter in the market. I was thirsty, and the afternoon seemed endless. Almost no one stopped, not even to look. The smell from the herring stall started to make me feel nauseous. The leaves of the carrots began to droop. Even the chickens were still.

"Can we go home now?" I asked Tillie.

"It's not time," she said. "Business always picks up later in the afternoon. You'll see."

It was late in the day when we heard hoofbeats approaching. Two horsemen stopped at the market entrance.

"What do you think they want?" I whispered to Tillie.

"I don't know. I just hope they don't want it from us."

"Me too."

We bent our heads, checking the careful place-
ment of our goods in front of us, but it didn't work.
A shadow fell over my things. When I looked up, I
saw two soldiers, dressed in the uniform of the
Czar's army. One of them reached out and picked
up the locket.

"Very nice," he said to his companion in Russian.

"It's all right," the other man said.

"How much?" he asked me in Yiddish.

"Four rubles, sir."

"What do you think?" he asked his friend.

"I think it's too much," said the other soldier.
"Those Jews are always charging too much."

My cheeks burned. The necklace was an old one
and real gold. It was worth at least four rubles. I
knew Mama wouldn't want me to sell it for less.
She'd said Minnie could keep it unless we got a very
good price.

The soldier looked at the locket in his hand.
"Well, girlie, what do you say?"

My mouth felt dry, but I managed to speak. "It's
four rubles. You don't have to buy it if you don't
want to."

"But I do want it. You people think you can
charge anything you want, don't you?"

I didn't answer. I just wished he'd put the locket
back and go away, without starting any trouble.

"Well. If that's how you feel," he said. He turned

suddenly. "Let's get out of here," he called to his friend. They walked quickly to their horses, jumped into the saddles, and left the market.

I was so glad they were gone that at first I didn't realize what had happened. Tillie was the first to notice. "Dvora!" she cried. "The locket. It's gone!"

We looked down, as though the locket would somehow reappear. "He took it," I began to cry. "He just took Minnie's locket!"

Tillie put her arm around me, but I couldn't stop crying. "He took the locket, the one Minnie loved so much. Oh, how can I ever tell her it's gone?"

Tillie patted my shoulder. I looked down at the stall. A few carvings and a shawl were left. "Why couldn't it have been something else?" I cried. "Then it wouldn't matter so much."

"Will your mother beat you?" Tillie asked.

"Mama? Beat me?" I almost smiled through my tears. "Mama never beats us."

"Well, you're lucky. My mother would almost kill me if I lost something worth that much."

"But Minnie will never forgive me."

Tillie shrugged. "So. What do you care? At least we weren't hurt. What if they'd taken us instead?"

I shivered. I'd heard stories of how Cossacks had gone through towns, setting fires to houses and taking young girls from their families. Tillie was right. That would have been worse, except maybe for

Minnie. She probably liked the locket more than me.

I was ready to go home, but Tillie said she had to stay until the market closed. She sold a few more brooms and I sold the rest of the carvings. Still the day was spoiled.

There was a weight of coins in my pocket by the time we left, but an even heavier weight in my heart. I'd have to tell Mama what happened and, what was worse, face Minnie.

5.

The Dream

It seemed hardly any time at all since the day Tillie and I first saw the Cossacks in the woods and Papa had told us of his plan, yet several weeks must have gone by.

Mama had sent a letter to Uncle Shmuel in America, to New York City where Aunt Sarah lived, telling them to expect us. We'd said goodbye to our aunts and uncles and to Bubba, Papa's mother, who lived in a little village a day's journey from our town. And we started to pack.

"I don't know what I'm going to do!" Mama cried one evening, sorting through the dishes.

"What's the matter, Esther?" Papa asked.

"We keep selling things and giving them away, yet the pile we're taking with us seems to get larger and

larger. We'll *never* be able to carry all that with us."
Mama pointed to the things in the middle of the
kitchen.

"Don't worry so," Papa said. "Just pack as much
as we can manage. We'll buy anything else we need
when we get there."

"But look at this teakettle, Jacob. Your mother
gave it to me when we went to say goodbye. We
can't leave *it* behind. Only it takes up so much
room!"

"So leave something else." Papa picked up the
soup pot. "Here. How about this? I'm sure they sell
pots and pans in America!"

Mama sighed. It wasn't just the soup pot. *I* knew
that. It was hard to leave *anything* behind.

While Mama sorted through our possessions,
Yossel and Minnie played with some bowls, stacking
them up and letting them fall over with a crash.

"I don't know what's the matter with you children," Mama snapped. She pushed Yossel to one
side and shook Minnie's shoulder. "You've been getting in the way all day. We'll never be ready to leave
tomorrow at this rate."

"Poor Mama," I thought. "Mama almost never
loses her temper. She must be upset about leaving
even though she hasn't said so. She didn't even
scold me that day I lost Minnie's necklace. She'd

just put her arm around me and said, 'Oh, Dvora. How terrible for you. I'm glad you're all right.' But Mama almost slapped Yossel just now."

We spent the evening packing. Papa took the tools he needed most and the ones he couldn't part with. Mama finally decided to leave all the pots. She took one featherbed for each of us, whispering to me that she'd managed to pack the old one I liked and the blue quilt for me too.

We would wear our second-best clothing for the trip, carrying our holiday things to wear when we reached America. Except for the kettle, a few bowls and clothes, some books and old letters, everything else would stay behind.

Late that night, Mama sewed our money into pockets she'd made into Papa's clothing and hers. "In case something happens to one of us," I heard her whisper to Papa, "at least we'll have half of it left."

"Very good, Esther."

"What shall we do about the children?"

"Give them each a ruble," Papa said, "and Shmuel's address in New York. That way they'll know where to go no matter what."

Mama gave Papa a look. "Not in front of the children, Jacob, please."

"What do you mean?" Minnie asked. "What could happen?"

"They have to know the chances, Esther."

"What Papa? What chances?" Yossel was listening now, too.

"Nothing's going to happen," Papa told us, "but something *might*."

"Like what?"

"Some of us might not get across the border."

"What's the border, Papa?" Yossel asked.

"It's the edge of Russia."

"Then why do we have to get across it?"

"We have to get to Poland and then all through Germany, to Hamburg, to get the boat that will take us to America. And it's hard stealing the border."

"Stealing the border?" Yossel asked. "What's that?"

"Well," Papa explained, "the Czar doesn't want us here, not really, but he won't let us leave either, especially not Saul, who could fight in his army."

"So what will we do, Papa?" Minnie wanted to know.

"We have no papers and we couldn't get them even if we tried, so we have to sneak away, steal the border into Poland. That's the only way that we can go."

Minnie and Yossel nodded.

"That's why I didn't want you to tell anyone our plans."

I wanted to ask Papa, "What if something happens

to one of us? What if we don't all get across the border?" only I didn't say anything. I was afraid. I'd never been far away before—not even to Berdichev or Kiev. Now we were going across the sea to another country. The trip was going to be more difficult than I'd thought. Just leaving was hard enough.

I looked around the room. "Do you suppose the house knows we're going away?" I asked Rivkeh. She was polishing the stove one last time. Everything had to be left spotless.

"Don't be silly, Dvora," she told me. "Houses don't know anything."

"But it looks so *different*."

"That's because we're all packed."

I wondered if Rivkeh was right. I put my hand on top of the oven. It was cold. The cooking fire was out for the first time in my life.

The oven had always helped us, heating the kitchen on cold winter evenings, baking Mama's challah, and warming the big pot of cholent every Friday so we'd have food for Shabbas. Most of all I remembered sleeping curled up on the shelf above it when I was three or four. "The house will *so* miss us," I thought. "I bet Rivkeh's wrong."

"Come, children, it's time for bed," Mama said softly. "We need a good night's sleep. Tomorrow's a big day."

The beds had all been sold. Mama spread featherbeds on the kitchen floor. "Good night, Papa, Goodnight, Mama," we said, kissing them. We lay down to sleep, close to one another on our last night in our house.

That night I had a dream.

I dreamt that Mama and Papa, Saul and Rivkeh, Minnie, Yossel, and I were riding in a cart, pulled by the enormous horses the Cossacks rode.

We drove for days. Sometimes we passed through villages filled with people, but no one seemed to see us.

Finally we came to the sea. It was so big I couldn't find where it ended. I knew it was the sea to America.

The cart stopped near the water. Suddenly the horses reared up and all of us fell into the water. It felt warm. The water was very deep and it began pulling at us.

Soon we were all far away from one another. I felt as though I were calling, "Help! Help!" only no sound came out. My parents and sisters and brothers drifted farther and farther away.

After what seemed a very long time, I looked up. I saw I was near land. My Uncle Shmuel and Ruthie's father were standing with their arms outstretched. They helped each of us out of the water and held us safe. Somehow our clothes were dry.

I woke up with a start. My mother and father were

talking near the door. It was morning and we were ready to go.

I helped Papa and Saul load our belongings on the cart: a bundle for each of us and a package of food Mama had made for the journey.

Before we left, I ran to say goodbye to Tillie.

We sat in the back, holding tightly to the sides, as the cart bumped its way along the road. At first it was interesting seeing the fields and people in different towns, but after a while we were tired of seeing the same things over and over.

One night we slept in an old barn, and another we tried to sleep in the bottom of our wagon. By the third day we were all tired of being cooped up and bumped around.

"Papa!" Yossel called. "Could we stop the wagon for a while?"

"No, Yossel," Papa said. "We have to reach the border as quickly as we can."

"I'm tired of riding," Yossel complained.

"Me too," Minnie added.

"We'll be there soon," Papa promised. "You should just be glad we've gotten this far without being stopped."

Minnie and Yossel quieted down. We all knew we were lucky. I wondered what we'd say if someone *did* stop us. Especially if they were soldiers! I hoped we wouldn't have to find out.

Minnie turned to Mama. "I'm hungry."

"I am, too!" Yossel said. Mama looked in the package. "There's not much left," she told them. "Just a few cookies. Papa says we'll be able to buy food when we get to the river."

"When will we be there?" I asked. I was hungry myself.

"Soon!" Papa called from the driver's seat. "We'll be there soon. Look! You can see the water way up ahead."

We drew closer and closer to the river. Papa stopped the cart near the edge. Tall grass grew along the bank. Behind the grass were bushes and a few trees. I could see the other side, far across the water.

"Everyone out!" Papa called. "All the bundles too!"

"But where are we going?" I asked. "There's nothing here."

Papa pointed. "Look," he said. "In the grass. Can you see the little house? That's where we'll stay."

I followed Papa's finger. Almost hidden by the grass was a straw hut. Did Papa mean we'd stay there? I guess he did because he carried our belongings inside. Then Papa climbed back on the wagon.

"Where are you going, Papa?" Saul asked.

"To the village. I have to find the man who's going to guide us across."

"Can I go too, Papa?" Yossel asked. "Can I go with you?" I didn't know why he wanted to get back on the wagon, Yossel was the one who couldn't wait to get off, but Papa shook his head. "No, Yossel. You stay with the others. I'll be back soon."

I thought being indoors after three days in the cart would be a relief, but the hut was terrible. It was dark and it smelled.

"Can we go outside?" Minnie asked as soon as Papa left. "We can play near the river."

"No, children," Mama told us. "You'll have to stay inside. We don't want anyone to find us here."

"No one would come here," I said. "It's awful."

"Sssh, Dvora. Wait till Papa comes back. We'll see what he says."

Papa didn't come back until late. Although he was tired, he was smiling.

"Is everything all right, Jacob?" Mama asked.

Papa nodded. "I found Peter, the man I wanted. He'll get us across the river and into Poland."

"Are we going now?" Minnie asked.

"No," Papa explained. "Not for a while. Peter says we'll have to wait until he has enough people. He doesn't go unless he has a large group."

"How long will that take?" Saul wanted to know.

"I'm not sure. Maybe three or four days. He just came back from taking another group across."

"Oh, Papa!" I cried. "It's terrible here. How can we stay that long?"

Papa looked around the hut. "It is pretty bad," he agreed. "Still, we just have to manage."

"What took you so long, Papa?" Yossel asked.

"Well, it was hard to find Peter. I just couldn't walk around the village asking, 'Where's the man who smuggles Jews into Poland?' could I?"

We laughed. "I guess not," Saul said. "How *did* you find him?"

"Don't ask! It was some job. And then I had to find someone to buy the cart and the horse too. But we're all set now."

"I'm glad you're back," Mama told him. "I was just getting worried."

Papa smiled. "Look what I bought!" He held up a package wrapped in newspaper. We crowded around while he opened it. "Don't worry," he told us, "it's kosher. I found a store run by Jews. I'll be able to go there every day to get what we need, fresh water too."

We stayed in the hut for five days and nights. It was awful, cooped up in the darkness with nothing to do. Papa and Mama wouldn't let us outside except to use the bushes. We took turns peeking through the door, watching the birds that hid in the grass or the changing shape of the clouds.

Once we saw a wagon stop and a family disappear into another hut. I hoped there'd be enough people soon. Staying here was terrible. I tried playing with Minnie and Yossel, but it was too crowded. The floor was hard and dirty. None of us slept much.

One afternoon I heard Saul ask Papa, "What if Peter doesn't come?"

"He'll come. Don't worry," Papa said.

"But what if he took your money and doesn't take us across?" Saul sounded worried.

My father shook his head. "I'm not so foolish," he explained. "I gave him half. Half here and half when we're safe in Poland. My friend Sol told me that's the way to do it."

"How did you know how much to give him?"

"I knew *about* how much it should be. He wanted a little more. I offered a little less. Finally we agreed on a price. I couldn't give him too little, could I?"

"Why not?"

"Well," Papa said. "There's an old saying: 'If you oil the cart, the wheels run smooth.' Peter is our cart. He's taking us to Poland."

As I listened to Saul and Papa, I chewed on the end of my braid. If Mama saw what I was doing she'd make me stop, but the hair tasted good. I tried to smell my hair instead of the sourness of the hut, only it didn't work.

Finally Papa left for town. When he came back, he had good news. "Tonight's the night," he told us. "Tonight we're leaving Russia." He looked around the hut. "Make sure everything's ready. Peter will be here after dark."

6.

Stealing the Border

We waited in the darkness in front of the hut. No one said a word. Other families stood in groups along the bank.

It was chilly and I pulled my shawl tight. I heard a rustling in the bushes behind us. "I hope it's Peter," I whispered to Rivkeh, "and not the border guards."

"Sshhh! No talking," Papa reminded us.

Overhead I saw the stars and the moon, the last time I'd see the stars of Russia. "Are the same stars in Poland? And do they have stars in America?" I wondered. Before I had a chance to ask Saul, a man stepped out of the woods.

He began walking toward the water, motioning for us to follow. We stopped at the edge of the river. "Not a sound now," Peter warned. "The guards have guns and we don't want anyone shot!"

Stealing the border suddenly seemed real, not a

game we were playing. If we made it, we'd be free, free from soldiers who took what they wanted without paying, free from the army, free to go to America. And if we didn't make it? I tried not to think about that.

"How are we going to get across?" I heard Minnie ask. "There aren't any boats."

"Walk!" my father told her, settling the heavy bundle holding his tools more securely on his back. "We're going to walk."

"Walk?" I asked in a whisper. "Across the water?" I remembered my dream of floating into space in the darkness.

"It's not too deep," my father said. "At least that's what Peter says. But we'd better get started now. We have to stay with the others. Roll up your trousers," he added, pointing to Saul and Yossel, "so they'll stay dry. And don't forget. The guards aren't far off."

All around were gasps and splashing sounds as people began making their way into the water. The group that had been nearest to us, three men, two women, and a girl about my age, was already quite far out. I could see their outline in the moonlight: the strangely shaped mass of their bundles, a small circle for their heads, and another longer shape of their body, cut in half by the water. It looked pretty deep to me.

"Come on. Let's go," Papa repeated. "And don't

let anything drop. If it falls into the river, we won't get it back."

Rivkeh and I stepped forward. My foot touched the water. "Aaiii!" I almost screamed. It was icy. How would I be able to walk through it?

I had no choice. In went my other foot. With each step I took I felt the water climb higher. It seemed even colder than it had at first. I pulled my shawl tighter in an effort to keep at least some of me warm. The river got deeper as we went farther in.

"What about our dresses?" I hissed to Rivkeh. "If it gets any deeper, they'll be soaked!"

"Try to hold your skirt up with your free hand."

"Free hand! I don't have any. One's keeping my bundle from falling into the water, and the other's holding my shawl."

"Well, just do the best you can."

We took one step after another. The cold wetness was up to my knees by now. "Poor Yossel," I thought. "I wonder how he's doing. The water's probably up to his *waist!*"

I felt the current at my legs, trying to pull me downstream. I kept going, one foot after another, trying to keep from falling, trying to stay straight ahead, hoping the guards were busy along another part of the river.

We were almost halfway across by now and no one had tried to stop us. I began to think we'd make

it, but my feet were getting worse. They felt as though they were turning to ice. At least the river wasn't getting any deeper now. I kept my skirts up as well as I could, hoping they'd stay dry.

Just then I heard a smothered cry from up ahead. The girl I'd noticed before grabbed wildly at her bundle. I saw her arm reach out, trying to save it. She leaned over as far as she could, but it was gone. The current had taken it.

The girl swayed. It looked as though she were going to fall. Then one of the women with her took her arm and led her on. I could see her, turning back, as if wishing her bundle would reappear.

I felt for mine again, making sure it was safe. Inside was my best dress, my two featherbeds, and Minnie's fancy one. That's all I'd have to do—lose something else of Minnie's!

Far off I heard another splash and a cry, only it was too far away to see what had happened.

We kept walking. The water was shallower by now and somehow less cold. I saw trees and bushes along the bank and hurried to reach it. At last we were on the other side.

I looked to make sure we were all safe. I saw Papa, Mama, and Minnie. Her skirts must have fallen into the water because they clung to her legs. Mine were just a little wet along the bottom, but my legs felt clammy anyway.

Saul and Yossel were the last ones out. "Oh, Yossel!" Mama cried. "What happened?"

Yossel was soaked. Water dripped from his hair, down his shoulders, and onto the ground. "I slipped," he said. "Saul grabbed my hand and pulled me out."

Saul had one wet arm across Yossel's back, but the rest of him was dry. "It's a good thing I was right there," Saul told us.

"Let me change you," Mama said. "There's dry clothing right here."

"We can't stop, Esther," Papa ordered. "We're not out of Russia yet."

"But the child's soaked."

"Never mind that. You'll change him later. Hurry now, children. We have to stay with Peter."

Mama wrapped her shawl around Yossel and we started off, following the others along a small path in the woods. Soon we came out into a field. It stretched far out in the distance. Stubble from corn scraped my legs.

There must have been forty or fifty people walking across the field. We looked like a strange market procession, lines of men and women, boys and girls, all of us with heavy bundles on our shoulders or backs, making our way together.

I saw the girl who'd lost her possessions walking slowly ahead of me. I went more quickly to catch up. When I reached her side, I could see she was still crying.

"I saw what happened," I said softly. "I'm sorry you lost your things."

She nodded to show she'd heard, but didn't answer.

"What's your name?" I asked.

"Naomi."

"I'm Dvora," I told her. "Are all those people in your family?" I asked, pointing to the men and women in front of us.

"No."

"Then who are they?"

"My uncle paid them to take me to America. I didn't know them before we left."

"Where are your parents?" I asked. "Are they in America?"

Naomi shook her head. "They're dead," she told me. "My father was in the army. He was killed before I was born."

"I'm sorry," I said. "What about your mother?"

"My mother and I lived with my uncle. Then she died when I was about five or six. I've been living with my uncle ever since. Now he says he can't afford to keep me. And he's sending me to another uncle in New York."

I couldn't think of anything to say. "I'm sorry," I finally told her again.

"That's all right." Naomi had stopped crying by this time. "I was scared at first," she said, "but I think it'll be better for me there. My uncle wrote that there are lots of jobs. He already has a place for me where he works."

"Doing what?"

"Needlework. He's in a factory where they make dresses and coats. He says they can always use a good seamstress."

I thought of Rivkeh. She sewed beautifully. Maybe Naomi's uncle could help her get a job. Unless Papa was going to find her a husband right away.

"What about you?" Naomi asked. "Are you going to get a job in America?"

I shook my head. "No. I don't think so. My father promised I could go to school. I'd like to be a teacher, only I don't know if girls can be teachers there." I couldn't imagine having to get a job when I was twelve the way Naomi was going to or like Tillie, who'd worked at the market for years.

"Girls can be teachers there."

"How do you know?"

"My uncle sent all his children through school. They've had women teachers—even the boys!"

"Oh, Naomi," I said. "That makes me feel so much better about going." She smiled. "What was in your bundle?" I asked her.

"My other skirt—I was saving it to wear when I met my uncle—my good shawl—it used to be my mother's—and a gift, a cloth I'd embroidered for my uncle."

"It's too bad you lost it."

"I know. It's a good thing the money for my ticket was sewn inside my dress." Naomi looked up. "At first I thought I couldn't live without it, especially Mama's shawl, but I guess I can."

We didn't talk for a while. I guess we were both thinking about America and what we'd find there. We walked through the field all night. Finally Peter stopped.

"What's the matter?" one of the men asked.

"Nothing," he said. "You'll be all right now. You're inside Poland."

People began to cheer and hug one another. The men crowded around Peter and shook his hand. They seemed almost happy to pay him their money.

"Town's that way," Peter told them, pointing the way we were going. "And the station's right on the main street."

Mama took out dry clothing for Yossel and food for all of us before we started off again. We were in Poland. The first part of the journey to America was over; the next part was about to begin.

7.

By Train across Poland

"Stay close together," Papa warned when we reached the station. "We don't want any of you to get lost." He found an empty spot on the platform and set down his pack.

"When's the train coming, Papa?" Yossel asked. He was so excited by the noise and movement that he could hardly stand still.

Papa shrugged. "I'm not sure," he said. "I'll have to ask at the ticket window."

"Can I go? Can I go too, Papa?" Minnie and Yossel shouted together.

"No. Wait here with the others. I'll be back as soon as I can." Papa carefully took some money from where he kept it hidden inside his jacket and went into the station.

I set my bundle next to Papa's, keeping one hand

on it to make sure it was safe. People kept walking by, talking loudly to one another. I heard Russian, Yiddish, and a language I didn't recognize.

I looked around for Naomi, but I couldn't find her in the crowd. "What if I never see her again?" I thought sadly. "In some ways it would be even worse than leaving Tillie. We could have gone to America together."

Just then Papa came back. "When's the train?" Saul asked. "Do we have to wait long?"

"It will be here soon," Papa said. "And I got the tickets. Third class!"

"But I thought you said we were going fourth class," Mama said, a worried look on her face.

"Yes, Esther, I know, only I met a landsman inside. He lived in the village where I grew up. He said third class doesn't cost much more but it's worth it. You can hardly sit down in the fourth-class car."

"What if we don't have enough for the boat tickets?"

"Don't worry. We have plenty. Just don't tell the robbers that!"

"All right Jacob. I'm sure you know best."

I looked at my father. "He'll always be able to take care of us," I thought, "even here where things are so strange."

As soon as the train pulled in, everyone started moving. People behind me tried to push me toward

it. The people in front pushed back until I thought I'd be squashed.

"Hold on to Yossel," Papa told Saul. "And Rivkeh, watch Minnie. You come with me, Dvora, we'll find seats for everyone."

Papa shouldered his pack and led the way through the crowd. It was easy to follow behind him. He reached out his arm and pulled me up the steps of the train.

It took a few minutes to get used to the darkness inside, but I could see it wasn't crowded. "Over here," Papa called. I walked to the middle of the car.

Papa had set his bundle down so that it covered two rows of seats facing one another. "Sit down," he told me, "before someone else takes them. I'll get Saul to help with the others."

We waited for the train to start. Papa sat next to the aisle, Mama facing him. Rivkeh sat next to Mama, Saul next to Papa. I was next to Saul at one window and Minnie and Yossel were opposite me. Right away they started to argue.

I leaned over. "Stop it!" I hissed. "Both of you! What will people think?"

"I want to sit next to the window!" Yossel complained.

"I was here first," Minnie answered. "Besides, I'm older."

"But I'm a boy."

"What does that have to do with it?"

"We're going to America because I'm a boy. That's why. Boys are the ones who have to get away from the army!"

"Well, I'm here and I'm staying."

"Ssshh," I said again. I was still afraid something would happen—even though we were too far away for the Cossacks to find us.

"I know what," I told them. "We'll take turns. You and Minnie first, then I'll change places with you." I moved over and took Yossel's seat next to Rivkeh. It really was too crowded for the four of us.

I felt Minnie's sharp elbow pressing in on one side, Rivkeh's softness on the other. It was a little better if I leaned forward. "At least Minnie and Yossel aren't quarreling," I thought.

The conductor shouted something I didn't understand, we heard a blast from the whistle, felt the train jerk, and we began to move. It was almost like being back on the cart. We sat pressed close to one another as we clattered along, only here Papa could lean back and sleep instead of having to drive.

Poland didn't look much different from Russia. We passed small villages, larger ones, and fields, fields, fields. When I got my turn at the window, I could see peasants cutting hay and picking vegetables the way they did at home. Only the haystacks were different.

Papa and Mama were talking. Saul sat reading a book. When I was tired of looking out I turned to Rivkeh. "Do you want to walk to the end of the car?" I asked her.

"If Papa says it's all right."

Papa smiled. "Of course you can. You won't get lost here. Take Minnie and Yossel too."

We squeezed past Mama. People filled every seat in the train. There were mothers with babies, groups of young men traveling together, farm people, and some families like ours.

At the other end of the car we found a small platform with a window. We could see into the next section. There weren't any seats in there, just two long benches down the middle. People stood propped up against the sides of the train or sat on their belongings.

"It's so crowded!" Rivkeh exclaimed. "I'm glad we aren't in there."

"That must be fourth class."

Rivkeh nodded. "I'm glad Papa bought third class. I don't know how we would have managed in there."

"Look! There's Naomi!" I cried. I waved, but she didn't see me. "At least she's on the same train. I was hoping I'd find her again."

"Maybe you'll see her when we stop," Rivkeh said, patting my arm.

I leaned against the side of the train. I could feel it

move and hear the clickety-clack of the wheels. They seemed to say: "Clickety-clack, clickety-clack: We're going back: We're going back." Only we weren't going back. We were going to America.

Minnie and Yossel were running in the aisles. "We'd better get them before they get into trouble," Rivkeh told me.

We passed another family, just about the size of ours. The mother was scolding one of the children. "He's pinching me, Mama," the girl complained.

"Stop whining," the mother said, slapping her. "Just keep still!"

The father was looking out the window. He didn't even seem to notice. "Children!" we heard the mother mutter. "They're more trouble than they're worth."

"Did you hear that?" I asked Rivkeh. She nodded. "She sounded just like Tillie's mother. I'm glad Mama isn't like that."

"Poor Mama. She looks tired," Rivkeh whispered when we'd reached our place. Mama had fallen asleep, stretched out along the wooden seat. We stayed in the aisle with Minnie and Yossel until she woke up.

Late that day Mama gave us the rest of the food we'd brought from Russia. "We'll need more soon," she told Papa.

"Maybe the train will stop long enough for me to

buy some," he told her. "We'll see. Tomorrow."

"I hope so. We need food. And drinking water too."

The train clattered on all day and all night. I slept a little, squeezed between Rivkeh and Minnie. Sometimes we stopped to take on more people, but it was never for more than a few minutes.

At one station a young boy got off with a water bottle. The whistle blew. Before he had a chance to get back on the train, we'd pulled out of the station. I could see him running, trying to catch up, and I heard his mother screaming, "Stop! Stop! Wait for my boy!" But the train didn't stop. I don't know if they ever found him again.

There was no outhouse on the train, just a tiny room at one end with a hole cut out in the floor. You could see the track rushing by underneath. The floor was slippery, and it smelled terrible in there. I hoped I wouldn't have to use it very often.

There was nowhere to wash and no drinking water either. The little water Papa had in the bottle was hardly enough. After a while everything was dirty: my arms with dark lines of soot, my once-white blouse, now spotted and gray, even my hair, although I couldn't see it.

We were all tired, hungry, and thirsty the next morning when the train finally pulled into a much

larger station. The conductor shouted something
we didn't understand.

"We'll be here half an hour," a Polish Jew explained.

"Good! That's enough time to buy food," Papa
said. "There should be plenty of places here."

"Can we go too, Papa? Please? Can we go?" we all
asked. "I'm tired of being cooped up on the train,"
Yossel told him. And Minnie added, "Me too!"

Papa and Mama looked at one another. I think
they wanted to say yes as much as we wanted to go,
but Papa shook his head. "No, children. You'd better not. It's too easy for someone to get lost."

I remembered the young boy from yesterday—I
wouldn't want to be left behind.

"I'll go alone," Papa decided, "and try to get everything we need."

"Don't buy anything unless it's kosher!" Mama
warned.

"Of course! Do you think I'd forget? I'll get bread.
That'll be all right. And maybe I can find cheese."

"Don't forget the water!"

We crowded to the window to watch.

Peddlers had set up stalls all along the side of the
station. A woman in a gaily embroidered red vest
and skirt sold meat pies. I'd never seen clothing like
hers before.

Several older women had trays of what looked like bread and rolls. They were round, with an indentation in the middle, not like the braided loaves we made at home. There were people selling tobacco, matches, cheese, cakes, even water.

Passengers from our train rushed up and down, trying to buy food before we left. Loud voices shouted in languages I didn't understand. Just looking at all the food made me hungry.

I saw Papa in the distance. He filled the water bottles first. Then he began walking along the platform. His black beard and long dark coat made him stand out from everyone else.

He went from one stall to another.

"Hurry, Papa, hurry!" I said to myself. "There isn't much time."

Finally he stopped in front of an old woman who had a tray of rolls. They were nice and dark, almost round. Papa reached out, squeezing one to see if it was fresh.

The old woman looked up and saw him. She said something to him in Polish. Papa didn't answer. Then, before any of us realized what was happening, she leaned over and slapped his hand. Papa dropped the roll. He couldn't say, "I want some food for my family. Are your rolls fresh?" She wouldn't understand him.

What would Papa do now, I wondered, shout, scold her, hit her back?

Instead, he ducked his head and shrugged. He pointed to the rolls and held out seven fingers. The woman nodded.

She counted out seven rolls and handed them to my father. He gave her a few coins, but she frowned and shook her head. He added more until finally she smiled and nodded.

All the while he kept his head bowed.

My father turned back to the train, just as the whistle sounded. He began to hurry, but he seemed to move as slowly as an old man. It was as though he'd been beaten by soldiers, not just slapped by an old woman.

After he sat down, Papa gave each of us a roll. "Eat," he said. "They're fresh."

I took what he handed to me. I had been hungry before but now I didn't feel like eating. When I looked at the roll, I could still see that woman hitting Papa. Finally I began to eat. I didn't think it tasted very good, but I ate it anyway.

8.

Welcome to Germany!

"We're coming to the border! We're coming to the border!" The news seemed to fly through the train.

Saul closed the book he'd been reading and looked up. Yossel pulled at his sleeve. "Tell me again, Saul," Yossel said. "What border is it?"

"Germany. It's the German border. We'll be there in a few minutes," Saul told him.

"Is that where we'll get the boat for America?" Minnie wanted to know.

"In Germany, yes," Papa said. "Only not here. We still have to take another train, to Hamburg. That's where the boats are."

"Will we have to steal the border, the way we did last time?" Yossel sounded anxious.

Papa shook his head. "No, no one wants us to stay in Poland," he explained. "And the Germans will let us through. That's what everyone says."

I hoped Papa was right. We couldn't be turned back now! Not after all we'd gone through.

The train stopped, but it wasn't in a station. We could see fields with crops growing and a village off in the distance. There were several large buildings outside with guards pacing back and forth in front of them.

"What do you think's happening?" I whispered to Rivkeh.

"I don't know," she answered, "but people are getting off. I can see them."

We watched the passengers filing into two of the buildings, men into one, women into the other. Just then the door opened and a guard motioned for us to get up.

He shouted something that sounded like "Out! Everyone out!" in Yiddish. People in the car stirred uneasily.

"What shall we do, Papa?"

"We'd better go. And take everything with you," he added, pointing to our things.

As we walked through the train I heard people asking, "Where are we going? What's going to happen?" But no one knew.

We followed the guard and joined the lines of people outside. Papa, Saul, and Yossel went into one of the buildings. Mama, Rivkeh, Minnie, and I filed into another.

Women in uniforms were at the door. They handed each of us a blanket, a towel, and a piece of soap and pointed inside. The room was filled with women from the train.

One of the guards ordered, "All clothing off!"

I wanted to ask, "Why? What for?" But the woman motioned impatiently with her hand and repeated, "Clothes off! Right away!"

Holding the blankets around us as best we could, we got undressed. There were no hooks for our dresses. We folded them and put them on top of the bundles.

"Come! This way!" The guard led us to the back of the room. It was made of tile. Metal pipes with water running from them came out of the walls. "Wash!" she ordered.

We had to put the blankets down. Rivkeh tried to keep her back turned, but there was no place to hide. It must have been awful for her.

The guards went around the room with a strong-smelling disinfectant. They put it on our clothing and the things in our bundles. The smell stung my nose.

By the time we'd finished washing, Rivkeh was

almost in tears. "Mama! This is so insulting. They must think we're dirty!"

"I know, Rivkele, I know." Mama tried to pat her arm. "Only by this time we probably are."

"But to make us undress like this—in front of strangers—it's not decent."

Mama sighed. "What can we do?" she said. "What can we do?"

"At least we had a chance to wash!" I told Rivkeh. "It's nice being clean again." And it was. The dust, dirt, and smell of the past days had been washed away. Only it would have been a lot nicer in a room by ourselves.

When we'd gotten dressed and collected our things, we were told to wait outside. I picked up my bundle. Everything smelled from the disinfectant they'd used. Even my hair.

Mama, Rivkeh, and Minnie found places together on a bench. I was just going to sit with them, when I saw a familiar figure.

"Naomi!" I called, running to her.

"Dvora!" she cried. "I was afraid I'd never see you again."

"I knew you were on the train! I waved to you from the other car, only you didn't see me."

"I'm glad we found each other again."

"Me too!"

Papa and the boys were done by this time. We

were just about to leave for town when a group of women arrived. They wore fine leather shoes and long, brightly colored dresses.

One of them made an announcement in Polish. Another spoke German. "Come with us," one of the women finally said in Yiddish. "We have food for you. We want to welcome you to Germany!"

"Welcome us to Germany? We just had a fine welcome!" someone near me muttered, but people began following the women to a large tent farther down the road.

"Come, children!" Papa called. "Let's stay together, Dvora! Saul! Over here!"

"Can Naomi come with us, Papa?" I asked.

"Your friend from the border? I don't see why not. Just be sure to tell her people where she'll be."

As we walked to the tent, we could see the town off in the distance. It looked about as large as our village in Russia.

The tent was filled with long tables. Benches were set up along either side. Naomi and I sat down together near one end.

The women began carrying in trays. I could see hot coffee, pitchers brimming with milk, and plates piled high with cake.

I could hardly wait. The last time I'd eaten was on the train when Papa bought the rolls. I hadn't enjoyed *that* very much.

I took a slice of cake. It was delicious: moist and sweet. Only it wasn't cake.

"Mama!" I cried. "Taste it! That's not cake. It's white bread. They're giving us white bread!"

Mama took a bite. "You're right Dvora. I've never tasted bread like it before."

"How do you think they make it, Mama?" Rivkeh asked.

"I don't know. Maybe a special kind of flour. It tastes a little like our challah, yet it's different. Only I don't see how they can have so much of it— enough for everyone on the train."

When the plate was empty, the women brought us more. We ate until everyone was satisfied.

"What people these Germans are," Papa said. "First they wash us, then they feed us. What do they think we are, children?" No one answered.

"Do you think they have white bread in America?" I asked Naomi.

She shrugged. "We'll find out soon enough."

"What do you think it'll be like there?"

"I'm not sure. Only I know it's big. A lot of people from my shtetl have gone there."

"I had a friend who went to America. I wonder if I'll see her again."

"You probably will. My uncle, the one in America, says you keep running into *landsleit* there."

"I hope I'll see you."

"I hope so too," Naomi said. I looked at my friend. She was all alone, on her way to live with an uncle she'd never seen. And she was just my age, maybe even younger.

"How old are you, Naomi?" I asked.

"Fourteen. How about you?" I was so surprised I didn't answer at first. I didn't want to tell her I was just twelve. Maybe she wouldn't want to be my friend anymore.

Naomi certainly didn't look fourteen. "Why, that's almost as old as Rivkeh," I thought to myself. "And Rivkeh's taller than Mama already." Naomi was a little smaller than me, skinny too with no hips or bosom.

"I'm almost thirteen," I finally told her. I hoped I wouldn't have to wait that long for my woman's body.

I was hoping I'd get it soon.

But Naomi could take care of herself. I'd seen that. I wondered if I could.

When it was time to leave, Naomi and I walked into town, to the station together. Papa bought train tickets to Hamburg.

"Say goodbye to your friend," he told me. "The train isn't until tomorrow. We need to find a place to sleep."

"Where?" I asked. "Here in the station like

Naomi?" I eyed the wooden benches. They didn't look very comfortable, but people were already getting settled on them.

"No," Papa told me. "We'll try to find a room in town."

"I'm tired," Minnie complained. "Is it far?"

"Not too far," Papa told her. "Everyone take your things."

We began walking down the main street. It was wider than streets in our village. Most buildings were larger and made of some kind of stone instead of wood and straw.

"Papa," I asked, "How are we going to find a place to sleep? We don't speak German."

Papa smiled. "You'll see."

We walked a little farther. Finally we passed an old man with a beard. He wore a black coat and a big hat like Papa's.

"Good afternoon," my father said to him in Yiddish.

"Good day, brother," the man replied, nodding his head.

Minnie, Yossel, and I wriggled excitedly. Maybe Germany wasn't so strange after all.

"We're from Russia," Papa told the man, "on our way to America. Do you know of a place where we can spend the night?"

"Follow me," he replied. The man turned the

corner. Soon we began seeing more men dressed like Papa. They spoke Yiddish too, only with a funny accent.

The house he took us to was the largest I'd ever been in. A sign, "Rooms to Let," was on the front door. Inside there was an enormous hall and a stairway leading up. It was the first time I'd been in a house with two floors.

Papa rented a room upstairs. It had three beds and was big enough for us all.

While Mama helped Minnie and Yossel wash and get ready for bed, Papa lay down and leaned back against the pillows. "Well," he said. "Things haven't worked out so badly, have they?"

"No, Papa," Saul and Rivkeh agreed. I thought of Yossel falling into the river, of the old woman slapping Papa's hand, of being tired and hungry. Still, we were all here. Safe. Together. Papa was right.

"We've gotten through two borders, been in three different countries," he continued, "The rest of the journey's easy. Tomorrow we leave for Hamburg. After that . . . America."

"Hamburg!" I said to myself. "The place from which boats sail to America." I tried to imagine what it would look like. I remembered the river we'd crossed coming into Poland. Maybe Hamburg was a big river.

There'd be lines of people waiting at the edge,

only instead of walking across, they'd get on boats. Then the boats would sail down the river to America.

"When does the boat go, Papa?" I asked. "When will we leave?"

"We'll find out when we reach Hamburg."

"I hope it'll be soon!"

"We all do!" Mama said, blowing out the lamp. "We've done enough traveling."

"Do you think it'll be tomorrow?" Minnie asked sleepily.

"I don't know. Hush now. It's time to get some rest."

It was good to be in a bed again, after spending so many nights sitting up on the train and on the hard floor of the hut. "Poor Naomi," I thought, "trying to sleep on a bench in the station. I'm glad I have Papa to take care of me."

"I wonder if she'll have a place to wash," I whispered to Rivkeh.

"Who?"

"Naomi. My friend."

"Ssh. You'll wake Minnie. Go to sleep."

Minnie kicked as she turned over. I lay still. Soon I heard Rivkeh's even breathing. My parents talked softly for a while in the big bed. Then they too were quiet.

I heard sounds from downstairs. It sounded like

singing, only I couldn't understand the songs. I thought I wouldn't be able to fall asleep, but I snuggled into the soft warmth of the covers. "Tomorrow will be a big day," I thought. "We're going to Hamburg and soon, America. I can't wait."

9.

Loss

The trip to Hamburg wasn't as long or as tiring as the journey across Poland had been. The train was larger and cleaner. Even sleeping wasn't bad. There was a cushion on the back of the seats to rest our heads.

There seemed to be more towns in Germany, and they were larger too. Sometimes the train waited almost an hour to take on passengers. At these stations, boys walked through the train selling bread, cake, and other food.

We pulled into Hamburg early the next morning. The station was enormous, with crowds of people on the platform pushing and shoving. At first we couldn't even find our way out.

Papa asked several people, but no one seemed to understand him. Finally the crowd cleared.

"We'll go into the station," Papa decided. "Someone's sure to know the way to the steamship office." He shouldered his pack. Each of us picked up our belongings.

"Where are we going now?" Yossel asked.

"To get the boat tickets," Saul told him.

"Is it far?"

"I don't know. Papa has to find where it is."

"But I'm tired," Yossel complained.

"Me too!" Minnie cried.

"You've been sleeping on the train all night!" Saul said. "You shouldn't be tired."

Yossel looked as though he were going to cry. "Come. Don't stop now," Saul told him. "We have to follow Papa."

The ticket office was filled with people. Papa found a man who spoke Yiddish, and asked him, "Where's the steamship office?"

"Which one?"

"The one that goes to America. We want to buy tickets."

"The one to America! That's all he wants!" the man announced in a loud voice. Several people turned to listen. I felt embarrassed for Papa. "Don't you know there are many different companies and each one has an office? There's not just one ship going to America!"

Papa flushed. "Well, can you direct me to the biggest one then?"

The man gave us directions: Walk this way, then that. Cross this and that street. It was very confusing, yet Papa seemed to understand.

"Thank you," he told the man. "Let's go," he said, turning to us.

"I'm tired, Papa," Yossel told him.

"I know, son. It's been a long trip. But we'll be there soon."

I hoped Papa was right, only it didn't seem soon to me. We walked and walked. My feet hurt and my arms too, from carrying my bundle. The streets were wide and crowded.

"Did you ever see so many beautiful dresses?" I asked Rivkeh, pointing to the women who were passing us.

She shook her head. "Never! They're even nicer than the ones the women wore at the border."

"Do you think everyone is rich here?"

"I don't know. They must be to dress like that."

People kept looking at us too. I guess they hadn't seen clothing like ours before either.

We saw elegant carriages ride by, carts with people from the countryside, and one or two very large wagons pulled by teams of horses. There were benches inside the wagons and perhaps twenty or thirty people sitting on them.

"Do you know what those are?" I asked Saul. "The wagons with all those people?"

"That's a street car," Saul explained. "They have them in big cities."

"Oh. I think I've read about them. I just never saw one before."

"I haven't either," Saul told me.

More street cars went by. They stopped at some corners to let people get on or off. I wished we could ride instead of walking.

Whenever Papa saw someone who looked Jewish, he'd stop them to ask, "Is this the way to the steamship company?"

They'd nod and point in the direction we were going. Yossel and Minnie were hanging onto Mama's skirts, complaining they were tired and hungry. I knew how they felt. I was too.

Finally we turned off the main street. We could see a sign with a picture of a ship on the next block. Minnie and Yossel raced ahead, forgetting they'd been so tired.

The office was in a large room. All along one wall were windows, like the ones at a train station. There were long lines in front of each one.

The rest of the room was filled with benches. Most of them were taken.

"Let's find a place for you to wait," Papa said. "Then I'll get the tickets."

"There's no place to sit, Jacob," Mama answered.

Papa looked around. "How about over there?" He pointed to the opposite end of the room. "There's an empty bench." We made our way to the back of the room. It felt good to sit down after such a long time.

"Are all the lines the same?" Papa asked a man who was with his family on the bench next to ours.

"No. They're all different," the man told him.

"What do you mean?"

"They're different. Different *lines*," he explained.

"But do they all go to America? I mean can you buy tickets to America here?"

The man nodded. "Yes. Only you'll have a long wait."

"I can see that. The lines are so long."

"Yes, they are, only after you wait on line you'll have an even longer wait for the boat!"

"What do you mean?"

"See all these people?" the man asked, waving one arm around the crowded room.

Papa nodded.

"They're all trying to get to the same place you are. The boat that leaves tomorrow was filled long ago. You'll be lucky if you get tickets for next week!"

"Next week!" Papa exclaimed. "We can't wait a whole *week*. We want to go right away."

"Sure. Just like everyone else. See these tickets?" the man continued. "They're for next week and I was lucky to get them. Someone told me he had to wait three weeks for a boat."

"What about one of the other offices?" Papa asked. "Would it be better there?"

The man shook his head. "It's the same everywhere. You have to wait. And this company is supposed to have the best ships." He picked up his pack, motioned to his family, and turned toward the door. "Good luck!" he called. "I hope you find passage soon."

We'd all been listening. Now we turned to Papa. "What are we going to do?" Saul asked. Minnie and Yossel began to cry.

Papa shook his head from side to side. "I didn't expect this," he told us. "I don't know what to say."

"We can't wait two weeks," Mama said slowly. "Not here."

"I know. We won't have enough money for that."

"So what will we do, Papa?" I asked.

"Let me see what the ticket seller says first," Papa decided. "Maybe that man was just fooling me. I can't believe the wait is so long. Then we'll decide what we'll do."

"Can I go with you, Papa?" I asked. Anything would be better than sitting on the bench listening to Minnie and Yossel, even standing on line.

Papa nodded. "Yes, Dvora. Come."

Papa and I waited and waited. The line hardly seemed to move. I was hungry by now too, but we couldn't get anything to eat. Not now. After a long time we reached the window.

"I want to buy tickets to America," my father said in Yiddish.

"For how many?" the man asked. We could barely understand him.

"For my wife, five children and me."

"You're paying rubles?"

Papa nodded.

"That'll be fifty rubles each," the ticket seller told him. "Thirty if they're children under twelve."

"I see. Could you tell me please, when is the boat?"

The man said something, but we didn't understand. "What?" Papa asked.

The ticket seller held up two fingers. "Two. Two weeks!" he shouted at Papa.

"Thank you. I need to talk to my family first. I'll be back later." My father and I walked back to where the others were waiting.

Minnie and Yossel were sitting on either side of Mama and Rivkeh. Minnie had fallen asleep, but Yossel looked as though he were still ready to cry.

"What shall we do, Esther?" Papa asked after he'd told everyone the story.

"I don't know what to say," Mama sighed. "But maybe you can find us some food first. The children have been cranky all morning. They need something to eat. And we'll be able to think better on a full stomach."

"You're right," Papa said. He took Saul and after a while came back with some bread and cheese. I'd

almost forgotten what it was like to have real meals, to sit down together at a table the way we used to. Here it was crowded and dirty. We ate anyway, the way other people around us were doing.

"Well, Esther, what shall we do?" Papa said again after we'd eaten.

"Maybe you should buy the tickets. We'll stay in Hamburg until the boat leaves. We'll find a place," Mama looked around the room with distaste, "even if we have to wait here."

"We can't stay here. Not for that long. And we'll need money for food. There won't be much left after we pay for the tickets. We need some money for America, too."

"I know, I know." Mama looked as though she were about to cry.

Just then a young man, dressed in the long black coat and hat of our part of Russia, approached our bench.

"Good afternoon, brother," he said to my father.

Papa looked up. "Hello!" he answered, smiling for the first time that morning. "A landsman!"

"Yes," the young man smiled back. "A landsman. Only I've been in Germany a few years. I ran away from Russia to escape the draft."

"Just like my boy here!" Papa told him, pointing to Saul.

"You look as though you're having trouble. Maybe I can help."

Papa shook his head. "I don't know if you can. We've been traveling a long time—across the border and through Poland—and we were hoping to get on a boat for America right away." The young man nodded sympathetically.

"I can see you'd want that! So what's the matter?"

"Now they tell us that the boats are crowded, that we have to wait two or three weeks. We're just trying to decide what to do. None of us want to stay here that long. Besides, it would be expensive. Maybe you *can* help, give us some advice."

The young man smiled. "I can do more than that."

"What do you mean?" Papa asked.

He leaned over. "I have a friend who works for the steamship company," he whispered. "They always save some tickets until the last minute. If you want"—he looked around to make sure no one was listening—"I can try to get passage for you on the boat that leaves tomorrow. Because you're a landsman!"

My father looked anxious. "Will it cost very much? We don't have much more than what we need for the tickets. But I'd be willing to pay a little extra, as long as we could leave right away."

"Don't worry. The tickets are fifty rubles each, for you and the wife, that's one hundred, another hundred for the young man and young woman." He smiled at Rivkeh, who blushed. "And thirty each for the others." He looked at me. "I think you'll still be able to pay children's fare," he said. "That'll be two hundred and ninety rubles. Better make it three hundred so I can give a little present to my friend."

"That's wonderful!" Papa cried. "It's almost too good to be true, isn't it Esther?"

Mama smiled back. She was as anxious to leave Hamburg as Papa. Papa and Mama took the money from where it was hidden inside their clothing. Papa carefully counted it out into the young man's hand.

"Just wait right here," he told us. "I'll be back as soon as I can." He smiled and disappeared behind a door in the back.

"It's a good thing that young man came along," Papa said, "or I don't know what we'd have done. There's still some money left, only not a great deal." He reached into his pocket. "Here, take this." He handed a few coins to Saul. "Take the little ones out and see if you can find them a drink."

The rest of us waited on the bench. It wasn't hard to wait, not now that we were getting our tickets. "We'll be going to America," I said to myself, "tomorrow, just the way we'd planned."

Saul came back with Minnie and Yossel. They began playing with some other children while Saul opened another book. He must have stuffed his pockets before we left! Rivkeh rested with her head against Mama. I was excited—we were finally going.

As the afternoon passed, people from the other

benches began gathering up their things and leaving. The lines at the ticket windows grew shorter. Finally a guard locked the front door.

"It must be closing time," Papa said. "That young man should be back soon."

"Do you think something happened?" Mama asked.

"What could happen?"

"I don't know—only where is he?"

One ticket window after another closed. Most benches were empty. When we were almost the only ones left, the guard came over. He said something in German that we didn't understand.

"What?" my father asked. "What did you say?"

"You can't stay here," he repeated.

"But we're waiting for someone."

"Not here!" The guard motioned toward the door.

"We can't leave now!" Papa sounded worried. "What should we do?"

"There must be someone who can talk to us," Saul said. He turned to the guard. "Can anyone speak Yiddish—or Russian?"

The guard nodded. He went to the back and returned with one of the ticket sellers. "What's the matter?" the man asked in Yiddish.

"We're waiting for our tickets," Papa explained.

"We're closed now. Why didn't you buy them earlier?"

"I'd better tell you the whole story," Papa said. He

told about our journey and not wanting to wait and about the young man who'd promised to help. When he was finished, the ticket seller looked sadly at Papa. I think I knew what he was going to say even before he spoke.

"I'm sorry," he told us. "You shouldn't have given him your money. There's no one who has extra tickets. Believe me. This ship was sold out more than a week ago."

"But what about the young man?" Papa asked. "And our money?"

The man shook his head. "I'm afraid he's gone. And your money too."

"Gone? Gone?" Papa repeated as though he didn't understand. "Our money to America gone?" He turned to Mama. She'd begun to rock back and forth.

"Oh, what are we going to do?" she cried. "What are we going to do?"

10.

Hamburg

We stood huddled in the doorway of the steamship office. I felt as though everyone was staring at us, wondering, "Who are those people? What are they doing here?"

It started to rain. I pulled my shawl up to keep my head dry. Mama tried to protect Minnie and Yossel as best she could.

Papa hunched over like an old man. We waited for him to speak, but he didn't say anything.

"Jacob," Mama finally asked, "what are we going to do?"

He shook his head. "I don't know," he muttered slowly.

"We can't stay here all night. The children are getting soaked. And they're hungry too."

Minnie and Yossel were so wet and tired, they'd

stopped complaining. Rivkeh stood next to them, waiting patiently.

Papa shrugged. "I don't know what to do," he repeated.

"Papa," Saul said, "we'd better do what the man suggested."

Papa looked at Saul as though he didn't understand what he'd said. "What?" he asked.

"The man. Inside," Saul repeated. "He said there were places to help people like us. Refugees in trouble, on their way to America."

Papa didn't answer.

"I think we should go there," Saul said.

"Yes, Papa," I added, tugging on his hand. "We just can't stay here."

Papa looked up at the people hurrying by. I knew what he must be thinking: "Everyone has a place to go . . . everyone except us."

It was dark, but we were able to see because the streets were lit with large lamps. They were on every corner. I'd never seen such a thing before.

"It's not far, Papa," Saul said. "We'd better go now, before it gets too late."

Papa sighed. He looked at us as though asking what to do.

"Saul's right, Papa. Let's go now," I told him.

By the time we managed to find the office, we

were all soaked. I was afraid it might be closed, but a woman was still there, sorting out papers at a desk.

She smiled when she saw us at the door. "Come in," she said in Yiddish. "Good evening."

"Good evening, ma'am," Saul answered.

"Can I help you?"

"I hope so," Papa replied. "Something awful has happened and we don't know what to do. We were told you might be able to help us."

"Come, sit down," she said. Her voice was comforting. "Let me get you a warm drink. Then you can tell me your trouble." She led us to a table. We sat down and waited until she gave each of us a glass of hot tea mixed with plenty of milk and sugar.

I sipped the hot liquid gratefully. It made me feel a little better. So did being inside.

As he drank his tea, Papa told her the whole story: how we'd left Russia, stolen the border, and come to Hamburg to get the ship for America. And about the young man who'd offered to buy us tickets.

The woman nodded sympathetically. "Well," she said, when Papa had finished, "there's no need for me to say you shouldn't have trusted that young man. I can see you know that already."

Papa sighed. "It was a terrible mistake," he agreed. "I only wish it hadn't happened. I don't know what will happen to us now."

"We'll think of something," she said briskly. "I'm sure we'll be able to help you." She went to her desk and began to write.

"Saul," I whispered, "do you think she'll help us get our money back?"

"How could she do that?"

"Find the young man and make him give it to us?"

"She'd never be able to find him—no one could. And anyway, how could we make him give back that money?"

"I don't know. Only I don't see how things will ever be all right unless our money's found."

The woman came back and handed a piece of paper to Papa. "Take this," she said. "And go to the address I've written down. You and your family will be able to eat and sleep there for a few days."

"What kind of a place is it?" Papa asked. "Will it cost very much?"

"No. No. Don't worry about that. It's free. It's run by the steamship company. They have beds there for people who are waiting for their boats to leave."

"I don't understand," Papa said. "If you have to wait for a boat they'll let you stay free?"

"That's right."

"Ohhhh," Papa moaned. "If only I'd known that! I would have bought the tickets and not worried about how we'd stay in Hamburg for two weeks. And I wouldn't have lost all our money."

"Never mind that now."

"But how can *we* stay in that place? We don't have tickets."

"I've explained what happened to you," the woman said, pointing to the note. "There'll be no trouble about putting you up."

"Oh, miss, how can we ever thank you!" Mama said. She squeezed the woman's hand.

"That's what we're here for," she said. "I'm glad to be able to help. You come back here tomorrow, after you've all had a good night's sleep. We'll try to help you decide what to do next."

We followed the directions she gave us and found several large tents near the edge of the city, something like the tent we'd eaten in when we entered Germany. Inside were rows and rows of beds.

The people in charge fed us and gave us a place to sleep: Papa, Saul, and Yossel at one end of the tent with the men and the rest of us on the other. We all had our own bed.

We lay down without bothering to get undressed. I didn't even unbraid my hair.

It felt strange to be in bed without someone pressed up against me. All around were the sounds of strangers sleeping.

I wondered what we'd do now, how we'd manage, what would happen to us. Papa had gotten us safely to Germany, yet now he'd made a terrible mistake.

The woman in the refugee office said she'd try to help, only what could she do? Our money was gone. Now we wouldn't be able to go to America. That was definite.

We could go back to Russia. Papa would open another shop and I could go to school. Only what would happen to Saul? No, that wasn't a good plan.

Maybe we'd stay here. Papa could work. But what about school? Saul and I couldn't go to school, not here in Hamburg.

I thought of my friend, Naomi. I'd hoped to meet her on the boat. But I'd probably never see her again. I used to feel sorry for Naomi. Now I had nothing too!

I started to cry, pressing my face into the blanket so no one would hear. "Oh, Papa, Papa—how could you lose our money? What's going to happen now?" I cried. "What will become of me?"

11.

The Telegram

The next morning the sky was clear. After we'd eaten breakfast together in the tent, Papa went back to the refugee office with Saul.

Mama, Rivkeh, and I straightened up our beds and took Minnie and Yossel outside. There was a clearing where the younger children were playing. Minnie and Yossel ran to join them.

We sat in the sun, watching the children play, waiting for Papa to come back. Rivkeh seemed to act as though nothing had happened. "It's easy for her," I thought. "All she wants is to get married, be a wife and mother just like Mama. Papa can find her a husband in Russia or America or even here. Nothing's changed very much for her. And Minnie and Yossel—they're too young to worry. As long as they have food to eat and someone to play with, they'll be happy."

I glanced at Mama. She sat hunched over, her head resting on her hand. I knew she was upset, worried about what would happen to Saul, to the whole family. I leaned my head on her shoulder. "Don't worry, so, Mama," I told her. "Maybe there'll be a way out."

She tried to smile. "I hope so, Dvora. We can't stay here forever."

"I know."

Children raced around playing, shouting in Yiddish, Russian, what I knew now was Polish and German, and languages I still didn't recognize.

They were dressed pretty much the same, but their parents wore a variety of clothing: short skirts, longer ones, brightly colored embroidery, dull gray dresses, kerchiefs, small caps, long coats and short. Many of the men kept their heads covered, either with hats like Papa's or with yarmelkes like Saul's and Yossel's. "I wonder what people in America wear?" I thought. "Now I'll never find out."

I saw Papa and Saul in the distance, walking slowly toward us.

"Hello, Jacob!" Mama called. "What did you find out?"

Papa was leaning on Saul. He looked smaller than he used to, somehow like an old man. He sighed and sat down next to us. "My head's in a whirl," he said.

"What happened?"

"There's so much to think about, I don't know where to begin."

"What did they say?" Mama asked.

"I spent all morning with the people in the refugee office. They say there are several choices."

"What are they, Papa?" I asked.

"I'll tell you—only none of them are good for all of us."

Mama and I nodded. We knew that already.

"We could go back to Russia," Papa began. "We have enough money for the train fare. I'd be able to open another shop and the children could all go to school."

"What about Saul?" Rivkeh asked. "Would he go too?"

Papa shook his head. "No. He'd have to stay here."

"Alone?"

"Well, I couldn't go back to Russia, could I?" Saul put in. "They'd take me right into the army."

"But if he stayed here alone, who knows what would happen," Papa said. "He might even turn out like that thief from the ticket office!"

"Oh, Papa. Don't be silly."

"That wouldn't be a good plan anyway," Mama said. "None of us want to go back to Russia."

"We could all stay here," Papa told us.

"Where?" I asked. "In the tent?"

"No. The people in the refugee office would help us find a place to live, and jobs. If we all worked, we could save enough for passage in a few years."

A few years! My heart sank. I'd end up working in a factory or selling in a shop. I wouldn't get to finish school. Neither would Saul. By the time we'd get to America it would be too late.

"Is there any other choice?" Mama wanted to know.

"Yes. They suggested that I go to America. I could live with Shmuel—that wouldn't cost very much. With the money I could make in America I'd save to bring you and the children over."

"Maybe you should do that, Jacob."

"Only how would you and the children live in the meantime?"

"As best we could," Mama said, but I could see from her face that she didn't like that plan very much.

"No," Papa shook his head. "I wouldn't want to leave you. Something might happen and we'd never see one another again."

"You're right, Jacob. It's better if we stay together. Are there any other plans?"

"That's just about it. We can stay here, go back to Russia, or one of us can go to America. Those are our choices."

I thought about what Papa had said.

All of a sudden he groaned. "Three hundred rubles. Gone. *Three hundred rubles.* It took me years to save it, the money to take us all to America."

"How much do we have left?" Mama asked.

"Well, we had about four hundred and fifty when we started. We've spent for the trains, food, and for Peter to help us steal the border. Let's see." He counted up. "There's just under one hundred rubles left."

"What do you think would be best?"

"I don't know. I just don't know. If only I hadn't given that man our money."

"It's too late to worry about that now," Mama reminded him. "We have to decide what to do."

We thought about it all that day. I heard Mama and Papa talking about what to do while we ate lunch with all the other people in the big tent. It was noisy there and crowded.

When a new group of people arrived, I looked to see if Naomi were with them. It would have been nice to find her again. To tell her what had happened.

We spent the night in the tent, that strange place that was beginning to feel like home. The next morning, after we'd eaten, Papa called us together.

"Come, children," he said. "We must talk. This concerns all of you."

"Have you decided what we'll do?" Saul asked.

Papa shook his head. "No, not definitely. Mama and I want to stay together. And we don't think it's a good idea to go back to Russia. We both want to get to America one day."

"Will we stay here, then in Germany?"

I thought of Papa's saying that we could all work, earn money for our passage, and my heart sank. Maybe we'd get to America someday, but it would be too late for me.

"Yes," Papa answered, "we'll stay. Mama and Rivkeh, the little ones and I. I'll be able to find work here. There may even be a job for Rivkeh."

"And me?" Saul asked.

"We'd like to send you to America," Papa told him. "There's enough money for your passage. You could stay with Shmuel and start school." He looked at Saul, who'd begun to smile. "That is if you want to."

"Do I want to! What a question. Of course!" Saul beamed.

"What about me?" I wasn't sure if I was thinking it or whether I'd asked the question that had been worrying me so.

All of a sudden I felt Mama's arms around me and I heard her say, "I think you should go too, Dvora. You need to go as much as Saul."

"But Mama," I asked, leaning against her, "what about the money?"

"There's enough. Fifty rubles for Saul and thirty for you. You're still small enough to pass for under twelve." She smiled at me. "And we'll have enough to get started here."

"Do you mean it, Mama? Papa?" I looked from one to the other.

Both of them nodded. "Yes, Dvora, we do," Papa told me.

"That is if *you* want to go," Mama added.

"Want to go? Of course I want to go. I just thought I wouldn't be able to."

"You know I promised that you could go to school," Papa told me. "Mama said that now we have to give you your chance."

I looked at Mama with surprise. I'd never known she felt like that about me. I'd always thought Rivkeh was her favorite. Well, maybe Rivkeh was, but she knew what I wanted, what I *needed*. How come I hadn't realized that before?

"So. It's decided?" Papa asked. "I want to tell the people at the office right away. They said they'd help buy the tickets so there won't be any mistake this time."

"What about you?" I asked Mama. "What will the rest of you do? Where will you stay?"

"We'll see what the people in the office have to suggest. They said Papa will have no trouble getting work—there's always a need for good craftsmen.

And they'll help us find a place to live too."

"Where will Saul and I stay?" I hadn't even thought of that before in my excitement.

"With Uncle Shmuel," Mama told me.

"Will it be all right? I mean will he have me?"

"I don't know," Papa said. "We hope so. I'm going to send him a telegram. To ask if it's possible."

"A telegram?" I asked. "What's that?"

"It's like a letter," Saul explained, "only it gets sent by wires, and it's much quicker."

"That's right," Papa added. "We should hear from Shmuel in a day or so."

He went off with Saul to tell them our decision and to get help with the telegram. I could hardly wait for the answer. It just had to be "yes."

12.

Crossing Over

"Did you get an answer, Papa? What did Uncle Shmuel say?" I asked as soon as he and Saul returned from the refugee office the next day.

"No, Dvora," he said. "We didn't hear anything. Not yet."

"Do you think something happened?"

"Don't worry," Saul told me. "It can take a while for a reply."

"But what if he didn't get it?" I asked. "What if he doesn't *want* us?"

"Don't be silly! Nothing happened and of course he'll take us," Saul said, but I was still afraid.

"You didn't hear the good news yet," Papa said. "I have your tickets—the boat leaves in less than two weeks. They were almost the last ones left!"

I hugged him. "Thank you, Papa." I didn't add: "I just hope we'll be able to go."

He turned to Mama. "And . . ." He paused dramatically. "We have a place to live."

"Oh, Jacob. That's wonderful. Where is it?"

"Near the center of town, a room in a big house. You'll be able to use the kitchen."

Mama smiled. "It'll be nice to cook again," she said. "I'm getting tired of other people's food."

"Can we see it?" Minnie asked.

"Yes! Let's go!" Yossel added, jumping up and down.

Papa shook his head. "No. It's too late. It's almost dark. I'll take you there tomorrow."

"Can't we go *now*? It's not that late. Please, Papa, please."

"No, children." Papa's voice was firm. "In the morning. We'll see if there's a telegram first. And then we'll look at the room."

There was no message the next day.

Saul tried to act as though it didn't matter, but I could see he was starting to worry too.

We walked through town, passing groups of well-dressed people. We saw more street cars. Some of them were so crowded that people stood, holding onto the sides.

Most of the buildings were large: four, five, and even six floors. I wondered how they kept from falling.

The place Papa had found was on a small street. It was much shabbier than the others we'd seen. The room was small. It had two large beds, a few hooks on the wall, one window looking out onto a dirty yard, a stand with a pitcher and basin, and nothing else.

Mama's face fell.

"I know it's small," Papa told her. Mama nodded although she didn't answer. "Once Saul and Dvora leave we'll be able to manage," he added.

"Wasn't there anything larger?" she asked.

"There's not too much to choose from. Things cost a lot here and this room's very cheap."

Minnie and Yossel climbed onto one of the beds and began to jump on it. "We have a room! We have a room!" they chanted.

"Stop that, children. Get down! You might break the bed," Mama warned. She turned to Papa. "Will we have to stay here the whole time?"

"I start working on Monday. We'll see how much I make and what it costs to live here. If we want to, later, we can always find another room."

"Maybe I can get a job too," Rivkeh added. "There must be people who need mending done. Or someone to look after their children."

"We'll look for something for you. The more we can save, the faster we'll be able to go."

I hoped the telegram would come soon. What if all seven of us had to live in that tiny space. It was hardly big enough for five.

We slept in the tent one more night. The next

morning we gathered up our things. Papa and Mama thanked the people in charge for letting us stay.

"We'll stop in the office on the way to our room," Papa said. "There's probably a message from Shmuel."

I was sure there'd be nothing, but this time a telegram was waiting.

I couldn't wait to hear what it said.

"SEND SAUL AND DVORA RIGHT AWAY," Papa read. "WILL MEET THEM AT ELLIS ISLAND WHEN THE BOAT DOCKS. SORRY TO HEAR OF YOUR TROUBLE. LOVE . . . SHMUEL."

The time passed quickly after that. The night before we were to sail, Saul and I packed. Mama had washed the clothes we'd been wearing for so long in the big washtub downstairs. "Who knows when you'll be able to wash again?" she told us.

Saul laid out his good clothing, his books, prayer shawl, and a blanket. Papa gave him six small bowls he'd carved in the evenings after work. "Give these to Shmuel and Sarah," he said. "Maybe they can use them."

"I'm sure they can, Papa. They're very nice." Saul wrapped them in the blanket.

Mama helped me pack my things. We put in the two quilts, my good clothing, and an extra blouse.

"Mama," I said, giving her a hug, "thank you for everything. I'm glad you took both quilts for me—I wasn't sure which one I wanted more."

"I knew you wanted them, Dvora." She hugged me back. "I'll give you Bubba's teakettle too, if it's not too heavy for you to carry."

"Can't you use it here? She gave it to *you*."

"No." Mama shook her head. "The kitchen's too small. You keep it for us until we get to America."

Her face fell for a minute, then she smiled. "Just think, Jacob," she told Papa, "by the time we get there the children will be real Americans. They'll be able to show us around."

Mama sewed our tickets and a paper with Shmuel's address in New York inside our clothing.

"Better give them each a few rubles too," Papa told her. "For America."

"But you'll need the money here!" I cried.

Papa shrugged. "We'll manage. And I don't want you to start out with nothing."

It was early when we left to get the boat. Hardly anyone was out on the streets. As we got nearer the pier, however, we saw more and more people. Everyone was going in the same direction.

I recognized some families who'd been living in the tent with us. A woman juggled a baby on her hip while a small boy tugged at her dress. "Hush! Hush!

I can't feed you now. Quiet, Louie, we'll be on the boat in a little while," she repeated, but the baby kept crying.

Near the edge of the pier a young man embraced his mother and turned toward the ship. "Wait, son! Wait!" she called. He looked back. "Take care of yourself!" she told him.

"I will, Mama."

As he walked up the plank leading to the ship, his mother began to cry loudly. "I'll never see him again. Never! Oh, my boy! My boy!"

"I hope Mama doesn't cry," I thought to myself. "*She* knows we'll see each other again." Still, I had a strange feeling in my stomach.

"You'd better go now," Papa warned. "It's almost time."

I looked up at the boat that was going to take us to America. The deck was filled with passengers. Men in sailor's uniforms stood about. Some were working on machinery in the front of the boat.

Suddenly I saw a familiar face.

"Naomi!" I called. "Naomi! Over here!" I tried calling her again. She didn't hear me because we were too far away.

I turned to Saul. "Did you see? It's Naomi, my friend. She's on the boat, the same one we're on!"

Saul nodded.

"I'm going to America with my friend!" I cried.

Soon we were together at the railing. I stood between Saul and Naomi, trying to find my family on shore.

"There they are!" Saul shouted. "Near the back."

Mama and Rivkeh had their arms around one another; Rivkeh held Minnie's hand. Papa carried Yossel on his shoulders. He looked taller again, the way I'd always thought he was.

"Mama! Papa!" I called. Saul and I waved wildly. Finally they heard and began to wave back. There was a frightening blast from a whistle. Men untied the ropes that connected us to the pier and the boat began to move.

We watched Mama and Papa, Rivkeh, Yossel, and Minnie grow smaller and smaller until we couldn't see them anymore.

I didn't know when I'd see them again, but somehow I wasn't afraid. They'd chosen me to go first. I had my chance now and I'd make something of myself. I'd become a woman in the country called America.

"Come, Naomi," I said, taking her hand. "Let's see what the rest of the ship is like." We turned from the rail and went inside.

About the Author

MARGE BLAINE writes for both young people and adults. Her picture book, *The Terrible Things That Happened At Our House*, was an ALA Notable book for 1975. She has reviewed children's theater for *The Village Voice* and currently serves as restaurant reviewer for a number of magazines. A native Brooklynite, Ms. Blaine lives in an old Victorian house in Flatbush, New York with her husband, children, and two Siamese cats.